STORIES FOR TODAY!

From the campus to a Chinese commune
to the wilds of the North—
Stories of the wild tumult of first love,
of the struggle to be accepted,
of rebellion in school, of cruelty, of the
need to escape from civilization into
strange worlds, and of the struggle
for liberty.

TEN MODERN AMERICAN SHORT STORIES

STORIES OF HUMOR, ROMANCE,
PATHOS AND ADVENTURE
BY TODAY'S MOST POWERFUL WRITERS

DAVID A. SOHN has edited several short
story collections including TEN TOP
STORIES and GREAT TALES OF HORROR
by Edgar Allan Poe. Mr. Sohn is Instructor of
English in Middlesex Junior High School,
Darien, Connecticut, and Assistant
Supervisor of Study Skills, The Study
Skills Office, Yale University.

BANTAM PATHFINDER EDITIONS

Bantam Pathfinder Editions provide the best in fiction and nonfiction in a wide variety of subject areas. They include novels by classic and contemporary writers; vivid, accurate histories and biographies; authoritative works in the sciences; collections of short stories, plays and poetry.

Bantam Pathfinder Editions are carefully selected and approved. They are durably bound, printed on specially selected high-quality paper, and presented in a new and handsome format.

TEN
MODERN AMERICAN
SHORT STORIES

Edited by David A. Sohn

Instructor of English,
Middlesex Junior High School,
Darien, Connecticut
Assistant Supervisor of Study Skills,
The Study Skills Office,
Yale University

BANTAM BOOKS

BANTAM PATHFINDER EDITIONS

NEW YORK / TORONTO / LONDON

RLI: VLM 6.0
IL 8.12

TEN MODERN AMERICAN SHORT STORIES
A Bantam Pathfinder edition / published November 1965
2nd printing
3rd printing
4th printing

ACKNOWLEDGMENTS

Paul Darcy Boles: "Night of Vengeance." First appeared in THE SATURDAY EVENING POST in 1960. Reprinted by permission of Russell and Volkening, Inc.

Pearl S. Buck: "A Field of Rice." Copyright © 1962 by Curtis Publishing Company. Reprinted by permission of Harold Ober Associates Incorporated.

Borden Deal: "Antaeus." From SOUTHWEST REVIEW, Spring, 1961. © 1961 by Southern Methodist University Press. Reprinted by permission.

James Jones: "The Valentine." First appeared in THE SATURDAY EVENING POST in 1963. © James Jones 1963. Reprinted by permission of Hope Leresche & Steele.

John Knowles: "A Turn with the Sun." Copyright, 1953, by Whit Burnett and Hallie Burnett; reprinted by permission of Whit Burnett and Hallie Burnett from STORY NO. 4.

Carson McCullers: "Sucker." Copyright © 1963 by Carson McCullers.

Reynolds Price: "Michael Egerton." From *The Names and Faces of Heroes* by Reynolds Price. Copyright © 1962 by Reynolds Price. Reprinted by permission of Atheneum Publishers. Also reprinted by permission of Chatto and Windus Ltd.

Jean Stafford: "The Scarlet Letter." Reprinted from MADEMOISELLE; Copyright © 1958 by The Street & Smith Publications, Inc.

Don Trompeter: "Bounty Hunters." First appeared in THE KENYON REVIEW. Reprinted by permission of Donald Trompeter.

John Updike: "A Sense of Shelter." Copyright © 1960, 1962 by John Updike. "A Sense of Shelter" originally appeared in THE NEW YORKER. Reprinted from *Pigeon Feathers and Other Stories*, by John Updike, by permission of Alfred A. Knopf, Inc. First published in Great Britain by André Deutsch Ltd. 1963. Also reprinted by permission of André Deutsch Ltd.

Library of Congress Catalog Card Number: 65-26667

Published simultaneously in the United States and Canada.

Bantam Books are published by Bantam Books, Inc., a subsidiary of Grosset & Dunlap, Inc. Its trade-mark, consisting of the words "Bantam Books" and the portrayal of a bantam, is registered in the United States Patent Office and in other countries. Marca Registrada. Bantam Books, Inc., 271 Madison Avenue, New York, N. Y. 10016.

PRINTED IN THE UNITED STATES OF AMERICA

Contents

Introduction

THIS IS a collection of stories by some of the outstanding writers of recent years. Several authors who have been awarded the highest honors of the literary world are represented, along with talented writers who should become worthy contenders for future honors.

Their stories are works of substance and subtlety. The reader will not find the vacuous "situation" story here, the cliché-ridden tale packed with cardboard characters, canned laughter, and instant tears. These are special visions of reality that have been translated into memorable fiction by gifted artists.

John Updike defined both fiction and reality in his National Book Award Acceptance Address, delivered on March 10, 1963:

"Fiction is a tissue of literal lies that refreshes and informs our sense of actuality. Reality is—chemically, atomically, biologically—a fabric of microscopic accuracies. The capture of such accuracies is the surest pleasure a writer receives."

"A Sense of Shelter" and the other stories in this collection reveal the keen perception and the knowledge of the writer's craft that illustrate John Updike's statement.

These are stories for the person who wishes to become a mature reader, or the person who may already have attained this goal. The mature reader perceives more than the surface elements of a short story. He appreciates the force and beauty of a superior style, the power of precise observation, and the subtle levels of meaning in symbolic or comparative prose. His reading enjoyment is enhanced by his grasp of how the author achieves his effects. He admires the craft as well as the art of writing. Reading intensively, he relates what he discovers to his personal experience and his view of the world. In an age where cheap sensations and distorted images bombard him incessantly through a multitude of media, he not only reads—which is remarkable enough—he *thinks* about what he reads.

These stories will offer him themes to think about, themes with which the young adult can identify. Rebellion against authority, the need for acceptance by a group, the bewildering aspects of early love, the majesty and violence of nature, the absurdity of bureaucracy, and the unquenchable spirit of freedom in the oppressed are a few of the themes treated by these authors.

There is variety in this group of stories—humor, adventure, romance and pathos. The descriptions that follow offer the reader an overview of the collection:

A TURN WITH THE SUN *by John Knowles*   This early story by John Knowles is set in the same school, Devon, that later was to become the setting for *A Separate Peace*. Lawrence Stuart, new to the school, inhabits "the nether world of the unregarded." His struggle for recognition and acceptance by the prep-school social elite forms the basis for a powerful story that vividly re-creates the atmosphere of a private school. It is rewarding to compare this story with *A Separate Peace*, for the light it sheds on Knowles' development as a writer.

THE SCARLET LETTER *by Jean Stafford*   Unlike Nathaniel Hawthorne's original, in theme and content, this "Scarlet Letter" is a comic romp with Jean Stafford's "bad characters," as she has called them. The adventures of Emily Vanderpool, an ebullient sixth-grader, and her "fellow," Virgil Meade, as they plot to outlaw geography homework, are engrossing and very funny. Jean Stafford demonstrates her ability to create appealing characters, to place them in amusing situations, and, with expert timing and a sensitive ear for dialogue, to write an immensely entertaining story.

THE VALENTINE *by James Jones* Those who are accustomed to his war stories will find this story by James Jones to be an unusual change of pace. It is a perceptive story about a boy in the eighth grade who has saved a lot of money to buy the most popular girl in the class a box of Valentine candy. It reveals the author's understanding of an adolescent's first encounter with unrequited love.

A SENSE OF SHELTER *by John Updike* Updike captures the atmosphere of a public high school with the skill that later created *The Centaur.* William Young, a senior, is bright, talented, shy and a stutterer. On a particular winter's day, he faces the problem of how to tell a girl that he loves her. The dialogue, the precise observation and the depth of characterization make this an exceptionally effective story.

MICHAEL EGERTON *by Reynolds Price* What happens to twelve-year-old Michael Egerton at camp reveals the callous indifference of the adult world. This is a subtle, delicate story by the author of *A Long and Happy Life* that shows how a broken home can affect a child.

SUCKER *by Carson McCullers* The narrator of this story is a sophomore in high school. When he is attracted to Maybelle, a very popular girl in school, his crush has a dramatic effect on the relationship between him and his twelve-year-old brother, Sucker. The result is a moving, bittersweet story.

ANTAEUS *by Borden Deal* The behavior of the entire gang is affected by the arrival of the strange and different "T.J." from the South. When he suggests that they grow crops somewhere in the city, the gang agrees to try it. This is a story of boys who try to make a world of their own in the concrete jungle.

A FIELD OF RICE *by Pearl S. Buck*   One of America's great writers here relates a tale of Communist China, of senseless bureaucracy in a totalitarian state.

NIGHT OF VENGEANCE *by Paul Darcy Boles*   This is a tale of life among the galley slaves and a plan to strike for freedom. Boles has created a realistic setting and the story moves forward with power and suspense. It is a compelling adventure about the oppressed, striving for liberty.

BOUNTY HUNTERS *by Don Trompeter*   Hunting wolves from an airplane is the unusual subject of this story. As the hunters find bounty, they also learn something about themselves. Don Trompeter's excellent descriptive style skillfully reproduces the North Country in twenty-below weather.

The section that follows discusses techniques for reading a short story and thinking about it.

ON READING A SHORT STORY

The underlying purpose for reading a short story should be to enjoy it. Cultivation of the enjoyment of reading should precede training in the use of formal analysis. If analysis is emphasized too early it can cast a pall on the reading of any type of literature. It is a better course for students to read widely and to determine for themselves why they like a story—vague as these speculations can be at times—than to be asphyxiated by a cloud of technical analysis that ends in the hatred of reading stories or novels because the act of reading has become a dreary exercise.

"The things I like to find in a story," states Sean O'Faolain in his excellent book, *The Short Story*, "are punch and poetry." If students can feel the punch and sense the poetry, their simple statement, "I liked it," is often enough.

But there can be value in intelligent analysis. If the teacher does not lose sight of the primary goal—reading pleasure—students can learn to appreciate the art and genius of a gifted storyteller by gaining a richer understanding of how he achieves effects. The *story* is what counts, but the shape of the story, the calculated plan of the author, yields a deeper delight if the reader senses the master strokes of the artist. As the reader learns to detect the craft as well as the art in a work, he becomes a mature critic.

The short story gives the reader a brief vision of life as one artist interprets it. Over a long period of time, stories form a kaleidoscopic view of human activity, a variety of perspectives for the reader. As insight is added to insight, his taste sharpens and his understanding of humanity grows.

Storytelling, an ancient art, is one of man's favorite diversions. A survey of modern media reveals numerous ways that man has devised to tell stories for entertainment—television, movies, comic books, theater, books, radio, magazines, to mention a few. Innate curiosity about what our fellow creatures feel—what they do and why—is apparently a universal characteristic. We satisfy this desire in complex ways that would have dazzled the Greeks who listened to the *Odyssey*. As A. E. Coppard once said, "Cut off a person from all contact with tales and he will assuredly begin to invent some—probably about himself."

An excellent short story reveals an aspect of reality filtered through the artist's imagination. Characters and human behaviors emerge in forms and attitudes that we have not perceived in quite the same way before. Insight, the "seeing into" life around him, is the gift of the gifted writer to his readers. We can feel the tension, the energy, the sensitivity of the artist as he distills his world into what John Updike calls "a tissue of literal lies" that we call fiction. The short story,

Sean O'Faolain suggests, is "an emphatically personal exposition," where the author selects a subject suited to his temperament.

The mature reader, therefore, is given the opportunity to plumb the depths of the artist's vision, discover a superior stylist, an excellent craftsman, a perceptive psychologist, a philosopher or a poet.

METHOD AND PURPOSE

Mature reading demands experience and perception. In the beginning, the two broad purposes for reading stories should be separated. Therefore the reader should read a story twice, once for surface pleasure, and a second time for study and analysis. (As he becomes a sophisticated reader, he may learn to combine the two readings into one appreciative experience.) The first "pleasure reading" will give him an overview of the story as well as the surface enjoyment of a well-told tale. He determines the relationships of the characters and discovers what happens to them. During the second reading, he searches for the craftsmanship—the architecture, the style, the mind behind the effect.

This two-pronged approach will not stifle him if he clearly discriminates between the two purposes. Some stories may not be worth critical analysis, and he may dismiss them with the first reading. But before the critical attitude becomes automatic, practice is necessary in reading as it is for any skill. The "twice-told tale" technique is a practical technique that eventually leads to the welding of pleasure and study. The reader should remember that the goal of critical analysis is, after all, a deeper appreciation of an artist's work.

READING FOR STUDY AND ANALYSIS

If the art of reading short stories well is the art of asking intelligent questions as we read, the first questions should be, "Are the characters believable? Do they smack of reality?" Flat, bland characters, the stock figures of fiction, cause a story to crumble.

The major characters in a story usually face a problem or situation that must be resolved. Unless there is at least one question that needs answering, there is no interest. When we say "the plot thickens," we mean that interest rises because of the intensity of our involvement with the unanswered question—the unsolved problem. A character involved in a dilemma catches our fancy. We want to know how he will extricate himself from the web the author has woven. The artist hooks the reader from the beginning with stimulating possibilities about the character or characters. Will Adam touch the tree of knowledge? Will David fight Goliath? Will Lawrence Stuart be accepted by the students at Devon in John Knowles' story, "A Turn with the Sun?" Will John Slade get a date with Margaret Simpson after he gives her the expensive valentine in James Jones' story, "The Valentine?"

The author selects his characters and their problems in relation to space and time. Hester Prynne of *The Scarlet Letter* would hardly face the same problem in a contemporary setting. Willy Loman, of *Death of a Salesman*, would be a different drummer in colonial Massachusetts. Verbal and social behavior are strongly influenced by where and when the characters exist.

The point of view in a story is significant. Why does the author choose the particular method of revealing the story? Does he tell the story through the eyes of one character and his reactions to other characters and events? Or does he play an omniscient role and relate the thoughts of various characters objectively? Does he use third-person narrative to present the story? Would Carson McCullers' story, "Sucker," be as effective if it were shifted to third-person narrative? Would John Updike's "A Sense of Shelter" come across as well if it were told through the first-person technique?

A brilliant short story reflects the art of compression and selection. The reader's interest is sustained by his involvement with the characters. Dramatic effect depends on the heightening of tension. The sequence of events is the element of structure we call plot. Tension ordinarily depends on *conflict*. Some sort of struggle, external or internal, is essential to reader interest. There are three general types of conflict: conflict between human(s) and human(s); conflict between human(s) and nature (or God); and conflict within the character(s), or what is called "internal conflict." Wang San's struggle with Comrade Li in Pearl Buck's "A Field of Rice" is, on a specific level, a conflict between humans and one person and a system. On a more symbolic level, it is the struggle of oppressed masses against the absurdity of a totalitarian bureaucracy. Don Trompeter's "Bounty Hunters" contains the age-old conflict of humans against nature as men hunt wolves from an airplane. John Knowles' Lawrence Stuart in "A Turn with the Sun" is a victim of internal conflict as the result of rejection by his peers, which is a conflict of human against humans. Stories may contain more than one type of conflict, but some sort of conflict is the seed of tension and suspense in any story.

Most stories build to a high point of tension, which becomes the turning point of the story. In classical terms, it is that point at which a moment of decision occurs. It is at this point that the fortunes of the protagonist are determined and the resolution to the problem begins. This point is called the *crisis* by many people. The climax follows the crisis. David's decision to fight Goliath is the crisis, and his fight and the victory are the climax. The alert reader searches for the turning point, or crisis, in the story.

A final question the reader should ask is, "What is the author saying about humanity?" The answer to this question—the insights the author offers us about his fellow creatures—is the *theme*. Eudora Welty has commented that "Human life is fiction's only theme." Elizabeth Bowen points out that great fiction relies on a few basic themes that "take color afresh from time or place." Whether the theme be the enigma of love, the dangerous delusions of pride or man's search for meaning, great stories put old themes in a new light and give us fresh perspective about others and ourselves.

GUIDELINES FOR ANALYZING THE SHORT STORY

The following questions may help the reader study the short story. Though not all questions may apply to each story, at least some of them may help the reader to think about what he has read:

TITLE

1. What is the exact title of the story? It is surprising how few readers can quote the precise title of a story they may have read a week previously.
2. Who is the author? This question is frequently difficult for the same reader who forgets the exact title. The absurdity of such forgetfulness is that if a writer has given us pleasure, odds are that another work by him would offer us more pleasure. Why not remember the author's name?
3. What is the significance of the title in relation to the story? Is it a title of irony? Does it sum up the main events? Does it state the theme?

PLACE AND TIME

1. Where does the story take place? Could it be as effective in another setting? Does the setting play a major role in the story?
2. When does the story take place? Does time play a major role in the story?
3. Is there a unity of time and place, or does the story change from time to time and from place to place?

CHARACTER

1. Who is the main character or who are the main characters? Are they believable?
2. Do the major characters change in any way from the beginning to the end of the story?
3. Are the characters consistent in the story, or do they ever act in an incredible manner?
4. Would you have acted differently from the way any of the characters acted during crucial points in the story?

Plot and Situation

1. What is the main problem the protagonist faces?
2. What is the source of conflict in the story? Is there more than one conflict?
3. How would you describe the conflict?
4. What is the crisis (the turning point) in the story?
5. How is the problem or situation resolved (the climax)?
6. Is there adequate suspense or tension in the story, or does your interest lag?
7. Do any of the incidents seem contrived and false?

Aspects of Style

1. What passages demonstrate the author's ability to draw sharp characterizations? What passages show that he has an ear for dialogue? A dramatic sense? A talent for imagery—that is, description or the creation of mood and tone?
2. Does the author ever use symbols? Foreshadowing? Repetition? Other literary devices, such as irony, dialect, etc.?
3. Are there any striking passages that you would like to remember?

Theme

1. What general truth does the author seem to be stating about human nature? Can you sum up the theme in a paragraph?
2. Do you agree with the author's feelings about humanity?

The Story as a Whole

1. Does the story have "punch"? "Poetry"? Explain.
2. Can you explain why you enjoyed or did not enjoy the story?
3. Does the author's writing resemble any other writing you have read?
4. What other stories has this author written? Would you like to read them? If you do not know what stories the author has written, where would you find out what they are?

David A. Sohn

A Turn with the Sun

BY JOHN KNOWLES

IT WAS dusk; the warm air of the early spring afternoon was edged with an exhilarating chill, and in the half-light the dark green turf of the playing field acquired the smooth perfection of a thick rug, spreading up to the thin woods lightly brushed with color along one sideline, and down to the river, with the stolid little bridge arching over it, along the other. Across the stream more playing fields, appearing smoother still in the distance, sloped gently up to the square gray shape of the gymnasium; and behind it the towers and turrets of the boy's school were etched against the darkening blue sky.

The lacrosse game was over, and the Red team, pleased by a three-to-two victory, but only mildly pleased since it was just an intramural game, formed a loose circle and cheered for themselves and their opponents: "Reds, Reds, Reds, Reds, Rah, Rah, Rah, Blues!" A few players tarried for some extra shots at the cage, which the second-string Blue goalie made half-hearted attempts to defend; but most of them straggled off toward the bridge, swinging their lacrosse sticks carelessly along beside them. Three boys played catch as they went; one of them missed a pass near the bridge and the ball plopped into the stream.

"Nuts!" he said. "I'm not going in after it."

"No, too cold," the others agreed.

As Lawrence stepped onto the gravel road which led over the bridge he experienced that thrill of feeling himself strong and athletic which the sound of

his cleets on a hard surface always excited. His stride
became more free-swinging, authoritative.

"I scored," he said simply. "D'you see that, Bead?
I scored my first goal."

"Yeah." Bead's scratchy voice had an overtone of
cordiality. "Good going, boy. The winning point
too."

They crunched along in silence up to the bridge,
and then Lawrence was emboldened to issue an invitation. "You going to the flick tonight? I mean I guess
it's Shelley Winters or someone . . ."

Bead balanced his companion's possible new status
for an indecisive instant, and then elected to hedge.
"Yeah, well I'll see you after dinner in the Butt Room
for a smoke. I'm prob'ly going. Bruce," he added with
careful casualness, "said something about it."

Bruce! Lawrence sensed once again that he was
helplessly sliding back, into the foggy social bottom-
land where unacceptable first-year boys dwell. He had
risen out of it just now: the goal he had scored, the
sweaty ease of his body, the grump-grump of his shoes
on the gravel had suggested something better. But
here was Bead, like himself only seven months at the
school, and yet going to the movies with Bruce. Lawrence marvelled at the speed with which Bead was
settling into the school, and he marvelled again at
his own failure, after seven months, to win a single
close friend.

Not that Lawrence Stuart was a pariah; the hockey
captain had never invaded his room, as he had Fruitcake Putsby's next door, and festooned his clothes
through the hall; he had never found a mixture of sour
cream and cereal in his bed at night, no one had ever
poured ink into the tub while he was bathing. The
victims of such violations were genuine outcasts. But
the very fact of their persecutions had, Lawrence reflected, some kind of negative value. They were at
least notable in their way. "There goes Fruitcake
Putsby!" someone would shout, "Hi ya, Fruitie."
They had a status all their own; and a few of them,
by senior year, could succeed by some miraculous

alchemy in becoming accepted and even respected by
the whole school.

Lawrence was neither grotesque enough nor cou-
rageous enough for that. He merely inhabited the
nether world of the unregarded, where no one bothered him or bothered about him. He had entered in
fourth form year, when the class was already clearly
stratified, knowing only one person in the school; he
came from a small Virginia town which no one had
ever heard of, his clothes were wrong, his vocabulary
was wrong, and when he talked at all it was about
the wrong things.

He had been assigned to an out-of-the-way house
(instead of to one of the exuberant dormitories) with
six other nebulous flotsam, and there on the edge of
the school he had been waiting all year for something
to happen to him, living alone in a little room tucked
up under the eaves.

His failure to strike out in some, in any, direction
puzzled him in October, when he had been at Devon
six weeks, angered him in December, made him con-
temptuous in February, and on this burgeoning April
day when everything else stirred with life, took on the
coloration of tragedy.

He crossed over the bridge with Bead, and his heart
stopped for an instant as it always did on this bridge;
in his imagination he again stood on the railing, with
his image white and mysterious in the green-black
water twenty-five feet below, and he leaped out and
over, as he had done last September on his fourth day
there, somersaulting twice while most of the school
looked on in admiration at the new boy, and knifed
cleanly into the icy water.

Last September, his fourth day at school. He hadn't
been thinking of anything in particular there on the
bridge; everyone was diving from it so he did too.
When he plunged from the railing he had been just
another of the unknown new boys, but when he broke
the surface of the water in that remarkable dive, one
that he had never attempted before and was never to
repeat, he became for his schoolmates a boy to be con-

sidered. That is why Ging Powers, a senior from his
own town who had seemed these first days to be de-
cisively avoiding him, came over in the shower room
afterwards and dropped an invitation to dinner like
a negligible piece of soap. "Come over to the Inn for
dinner tonight. Got a couple of friends I want you to
meet."

There is a trophy room in the Devon School gymnasium much visited by returning alumni; during June
reunions they wander whispering past its softly lighted cases, in which gleam the cups and medals of athletic greatness. Proud banners hang from its panelled
walls, inscribed with the records of triumphant, forgotten afternoons. It is like a small, peculiarly sacred
chapel in a great cathedral.

At the far end, standing long and bright in the focal
niche, the alumni would admire the James Harvey
Fullerton Cup, Awarded Each Year to That Member
of the Sixth Form Who, in the Opinion of his Fellows and Masters, Most Closely Exemplifies the Highest Traditions of Devon. There is no mention of athletics on the inscription, but it has come to rest in the
gymnasium, in the place of honor, because the highest
tradition of Devon is the thinking athlete. Thirty-four
names have been engraved on its burnished surface
since Mr. Fullerton, feeling disturbed by the activities
of German submarines, decided to confirm the reality
of his untroubled childhood by donating it, with a
small endowment, to his old school, like some symbol
of royalty.

Lawrence had approached it that afternoon, his
fourth day at the school, and was struck by the beauty
and sacredness of the place. This surely was the heart
of Devon: the chapel was like an assembly hall, the
library was a clearing house, the houses were dormitories, the classrooms, classrooms; only here did he
sense that behind the visible were deeper meanings,
that these trophies and banners were clues to the hidden core of the school. He left the gymnasium lost
in thought.

He had felt he was still in the air as he walked from the gym back to his room that afternoon, still spinning down upon his own bright image in the murky water. He dressed hurriedly for the dinner at the Inn, for this was surely the beginning of his career at Devon. He explained how wonderfully everything was going in an ardent letter to Janine, and then walked, holding himself back from running by an intoxicating exercise of will power, and arrived at last at the Inn. Everything within him was released; it was as though his dive into the river had washed away his boyhood, and he stood clean and happy, wondering dreamily what he would be like now.

The hushed dining room was pervaded by the atmosphere of middle-aged gentility characteristic of Inns at boys' schools: the dull walnut woodwork, the pink and green wallpaper depicting Colonial scenes, the virginal fireplace. At the far end of the room Lawrence saw his dinner partners huddled conspiratorily at a corner table. He wheeled past other, empty tables, bright with white cloths and silver, realized dimly that there were murmuring groups dining here and there in the room; and then Ging, his thin frame unfolding from a chair, was muttering introductions. "This is Vinnie Ump," he seemed to say, and Lawrence recognized Vinnie James, vice-chairman of the senior council, a calm, blond Bostonian who was allowed to be as articulate as he chose because he was so unassertively sure of himself. "And this," said Ging, in a somewhat more stately cadence, "is Charles Morrell." Lawrence recognized him too, of course; this was Morrell, the fabled "Captain Marvel" of the football field, the baseball field, and the hockey rink. Lawrence had never seen him at close quarters before; he seemed more formidable than ever.

Vinnie James was talking, and after pausing for a neutral, bird-like nod to Lawrence, he continued. "So if you want to put up with being patronized by a lot of crashing bores, then you can go to Harvard, and be Punched all sophomore year."

Captain Marvel leaned his heavily handsome face

out over the table, "I don't get you, Vinnie, what's this Punching?"

"That's how you get into the clubs at Harvard, Dim One," Vinnie's eyes flickered humorously at him for an instant. "They invite you to Punch parties all sophomore year, and when they stop inviting you then you know you're not going to be asked to join the club."

"Well," Ging looked with masked apprehension from one to the other, "they've got to take *some* guys, don't they? And Devon isn't such a bad background."

"It's not Groton," said Vinnie mercilessly, "of course."

"Groton!" Ging clutched his tastefully striped tie savagely. "I wouldn't be caught dead at that snobatorium. I could 'ev', if I'd wanted to I could 'ev' gone to Groton. But mother said wild horses couldn't drag a son of hers to that snobatorium."

Lawrence felt dizzy at the barefaceness of this lie. He knew that Mrs. Powers would cheerfully have violated most of the customs of civilization to get a son of hers into Groton. Devon had been a hasty compromise after Groton had proved out of the question.

"In any case," Vinnie remarked drily, "Marvel here won't have any trouble. Personable athletes are kidnapped by the most desirable clubs the moment they appear." Vinnie made no comment on Ging's chances.

Lawrence disliked and felt superior to Ging at once. The climber! He had never realized before what a fool Ging was, it made him feel older to realize it now. It was so clear when you could see him beside Captain Marvel, cool, unconcerned Marvel, who would easily rise to the top of every group he entered, leaving Ging clawing and snarling below.

Lawrence looked away irritably, regretting that it was Ging who had introduced him to the others. At the same time he felt himself more thoroughly aware than he had ever been of how the world went, of who fitted where, of what was grand and genuine and what was shoddy and fake. Devon had posed a question to him, and demanded that he do something. This after-

noon he had done a single, beautiful dive, it was just
right and he knew it the moment he hit the water.
And now he had come to understand Captain Marvel.
The answer was athletics; not just winning a major
D, but the personality of the athlete itself, the un-
conscious authority which his strength, his skill, his
acclaim gave him. Lawrence stirred his tomato soup
reflectively, and felt his diffuse ambitions coming into
focus, experienced a vision of himself as the Majestic
Athlete; he decided instinctively and immediately to
accept it, there at dinner among the walnut and silver
and the polite murmurings of the other diners. He
gathered about himself the mantle of the Olympiad,
and lost in its folds, he burst into speech.

"I have some cousins, two cousins, you know, Ging
—George and Carter—they're in clubs at Harvard, I
mean a club at Harvard, one club, both of 'em are in
the same club. It's the . . . the . . ." Lawrence was
suddenly stricken with the thought that George and
Carter might very easily not be in the best Harvard
club, or even the second best; but everyone, even Marvel, was listening with interest, "It's called," he felt
his color rising at the inelegance of the name, "The
Gas—or something."

"Oh yes," said Vinnie crisply, "that's a very good
club, for New Yorkers mostly, they have some very
good men."

"Oh," Lawrence breathed with fake innocence and
real relief. This success swept him spinning on.
"George and Carter, they go there for dinners, but
they always have lunch in the—is it the Houses?" his
wide, brightened blue eyes searched his listeners faces
avidly; Vinnie nodded a brief assent. "They said those
clubs make you so ingrown, you just know all these
fancy socialites and everything and they wanted to
know, you know, everybody, they didn't want to be
exclusive or anything like that. It isn't like up here, I
mean there isn't, aren't all these clubs and things. They
said that I'd get raided and my bed peed and all but
nothing like that seems to happen up here; but they
did say that when I went on to Harvard, if I do go

there, that after being here it'll be easier and I'll know
people and not have to study, but I don't really study
so hard here, 'course it's only been four days, but
after what everybody said about prep school I thought
I'd be studying all the time, but, well, take this afternoon"—that was good, *take this afternoon* smacked
of maturity; he paused an instant for the two important seniors (Ging was a bystander now) to catch the
overtone of authority in it—"we went swimming off
the bridge, and that flip, I thought a two-and-a-half
flip might be tough, but . . ." he paused again, hoping
Ging might make himself useful as a witness to this
feat; nothing happened so he finished a little out of
breath, "it wasn't."

"Yeah," Captain Marvel said, "I saw you do it."

This swept down Lawrence's last controls. His best
moment had been seen, and doubtless admired, by the
most important athlete in school. He rushed ahead
now, eager to impress him even more; no, by golly, he
was through impressing people. Now he was ready to
leap, in one magnificent bound, to the very peak of
his ambitions, to become Captain Marvel's protegé, to
learn what it meant to be unconcerned, powerful, and
a man. So he stuttered gaily on, snatching at everything inside him that seemed presentable—home, his
family, Janine, the play he had seen in New York; he
assumed every grown-up attitude he could find. All
of it he brought forth, as an offering of fealty.

The seniors followed this unwinding of a new boy
carefully, looked where he pointed, gauging all his in-
formation and attitudes according to their own more
precisely graded yardsticks, and took his measure.

"Devon is like some kind of country club-peniten-
tiary, where the inmates don't take walks around the
courtyard, they go to the private penitentiary golf
course for eighteen holes. And the dean, is that who
he is? that queer, stuttery old bird, you know, the one
in chapel the first day, the one who looks like Hoover
with an Oxford accent . . ."

"Yes, that's the dean," said Vinnie, fingering his
water glass, "Dean Eleazer Markham Bings-Smith."

"No!" exploded Lawrence, "is that his name! His honest name?" He regretted the *honest*, it should have been *actual*.

"Why does he talk that way, and *look* that way! Like my beagle, that's the way he looks, like the beagle I've got at home, my beagle looks just like that right after he's had a bath."

There was something like consternation passing around the table. Lawrence felt it and looked wonderingly from one to the other. Ging was watching an elderly couple making their way toward the door. The others examined their desserts.

"Was that the dean?" Lawrence asked in a shocked whisper. "Did he hear me?"

No one really answered, but Lawrence, alive in every nerve now, responded symbolically. He slipped like a boneless organism from his chair and sank beneath the table; there he performed the appropriate expiation; he banged his head, not too hard, against the table's underside.

There was a scraping of chairs, Lawrence saw napkins flutter onto the seats, and suddenly he realized the impossibility of his position: under a table in the Anthony Wayne Dining Room of the Devon Inn, making a fool of himself.

He could not recall afterwards how he got to his feet, but he remembered very clearly what was said.

"I have an appointment," Vinnie was informing Ging, and then to Lawrence, "That was not the dean, that was Dr. Farnham, the registrar. I doubt whether he heard you. And if he did, I doubt whether he knows or cares *who* you are."

"Are you British?" demanded Captain Marvel with heavy distaste. "Is that why you talk so queer?"

Lawrence felt the exuberance within him turn over, leaving a sob pressing against his chest. He could not speak and would not cry, but drew a deep, shuddering breath.

Marvel and Vinnie strode out through the door, Ging followed, and Lawrence roamed out a few paces behind, out into the damp September night, down the deserted street to the quadrangle, where the dormitory lights streamed hospitably from cozy windows. Ging said "G'night" there as though he were saying "pass" during a dull bridge game, and Lawrence was left to wander down the lane to the cluttered old house, to the little room stuck up under the eaves where he lived.

In the next weeks, after the first storms had subsided, Lawrence tried again and again to analyze his failure. Whom had he offended, how, why? Why was everything he had ever wanted sparkling like a trophy in his hands one minute, and smashed to bits at his feet the next?

Defeat seemed to follow upon defeat after that. Having missed the peak of his ambition, he assumed that lesser heights could be attained automatically; he felt like a veteran of violent foreign wars whose scars entitled him to homage and precedence. Instead he was battered on every occasion: one day he offered to move into the empty half of a double room down the hall and the boy living there had simply ignored him, had pretended not to hear. Then he turned wildly delinquent; he threw his small steamer trunk, filled with shoes and books, down the long flight of stairs under which the housemaster lived. It slammed against Mr. Kazusk's door at the bottom, and the resultant methodical investigation and punishment made him briefly notable to his housemates, until they concluded that he was strange.

This was the final, the unbearable affront; they thought him strange, undisciplined, an inferior little boy given to pettish tantrums. He would show them. If there was one thing he was sure he possessed, it was a capacity for self-discipline. If there was one thing he would not be, it was a clown, a butt. He knew there was a certain dignity in his bearing, even though it shaded into pomposity, and he would not violate that, he would not become a Fruitcake Putsby, even if people would like him better that way.

He decided, in the season when the last leaves were

drifting down from the trees bordering the playing fields, and the sunlight cut obliquely across the town, that there remained this one quality on which he could rely: his capacity for self-discipline. He would turn his back upon the school, he would no longer be embroiled in Devon's cheap competition for importance. He would be intelligent; yes, he told himself, he would be *exceedingly* intelligent; and by God, if he only could, he would be the greatest athlete ever to electrify a crowd on the playing fields of Devon. The greatest, and the most inaccessible.

The earth was turning wintery; the season of Steam Heat arrived. It filled every inhabited room in the school, the steam hissed and clanged with power, and could not be shut off. Slowly the heat drained the spirit from them, dried their healthy faces, sered the freshest skin. The usual number of colds appeared, the usual amount of force faded from lectures and application from homework, the usual apathy slipped into the school through the radiators. Winter was here.

Lawrence moved from one steaming box to another, crossing the sharp, drily cold outdoors in between, and felt his own inner strength grow as it waned in those about him. He had learned to study very systematically, and his responses in class were apt and laconic, several of his teachers became noticeably interested in winning his good opinion; they would make remarks about Kafka or Turgenev and then glance at him. He would smile knowingly back, and resolve to find out who these people might be.

His free time he spent watching athletics, religiously following the major sports, football games and football drill, enjoying every moment except when Captain Marvel made a really brilliant play, which made him feel uneasy and guilty. He watched soccer and track and tennis and squash, and as winter sports replaced them, he watched basketball, wrestling, boxing, hockey, and even fencing.

In the fall he had played a little intramural football at which he was generally inept and abstracted, but

once in a while he would startle everyone, including
himself, with a brilliantly skillful play. But there was
too much freedom on a football field, too much room
to maneuver, too many possibilities; so in the winter
he turned to swimming, in which the lanes were rigid-
ly predetermined, and he had only to swim up and
down, up and down. Into this he poured all the intensity he possessed, and as a result made the junior varsity squad. He was uniformly cooperative with his
teammates, and the coach thought him a promising
boy.

His housemates now felt disposed to revise their
opinion of him; yes, Stuart was strange, but if he was
going to turn out to be not only bright but also something of an athlete, they thought they had better accept him.

The proctor and the others made a few fumbling,
gruff overtures. Lawrence sensed this at once and became more thoroughly disturbed than at any time
since the dinner at the inn. He loathed them all, of
course, and he felt cheated; now that his defenses were
invulnerable they were calling off the assault, inviting
him to talk terms, asking for a conference out in the
open. The cold wind tore around the angles of the old
house, and Lawrence camped in his steamy room,
speaking politely to those who came to his door, doing
his homework, and feeling confusedly vindicated. He
had proved the strongest of all, for what was strength
if not the capacity for self-denial? He had divorced
himself from them so successfully that now he didn't
care; *they* cared, so it seemed, now; they were seeking
his friendship, therefore they were weak. Strength,
Lawrence was sure, was the capacity for self-denial;
life was conquered by the strong-willed, success was
demonstrated by austerity; it was the bleak who would
inherit the earth. Yes, that was right and he would
not allow them to change the rules now that he had
won; he decided to continue his triumphant game,
even though he was playing it alone.

Only in his anger did he draw close to them; one
dismal afternoon in February Billy Baldwin, the boy

down the hall who had refused to room with him in September, came to his door:

"Hi, Varsity." This was the nickname Lawrence had been given by the other boys, who understood him better than he thought. "You going to Bermuda for spring vacation?" Since he was excluded from the gay round of parties which the boys from Boston and New York described as typical of their holidays, Lawrence had intimated that he was going to Bermuda with his family. This afternoon he was too depressed to lie.

"No," he parroted, "I'm not going to Bermuda for spring vacation."

Billy was a little put off, but continued with determined good humor. "Well then how about coming down, I mean if you aren't going home . . ." Billy had no champagne vacation in the offing either, but he had grown up a little during the winter and forgiven his parents for making their home in Bridgeport, Connecticut. He had also changed his mind about Lawrence, whom he now thought pleasantly temperamental and handsome. "Why don't you, if you want, you could always . . ."

"What?" interrupted Lawrence irritably. "Why don't I what?"

"All I was going to say," Billy continued on a stronger note, "what I was going to say if you didn't interrupt all the time . . ." but then he couldn't say it.

"You were going to say nothing," Lawrence said disgustedly, turning back to his book, "as usual."

"Just one thing," Billy exclaimed sharply, "All I was going to say was why *don't* you go to Bermuda? If you're so rich."

"Rich enough," Lawrence's voice thickening with controlled anger, "Richer than some people who live in little dump towns on the New Haven Railroad."

"Yeah!" Billy shouted. "Yeah, so rich your pop couldn't pay the last bursar's bill on time!"

"What!" screamed Lawrence, tearing the book from his lap and jumping up, "Wha'd you say?" His blood was pounding because it wasn't the truth, but it was close to it. He was standing now in the middle of his little garret, his shoulders slightly forward. His voice turned coarse, "Get out." Neither of them knew his voice had a savage depth like that. "Just get out of my room." Then in a single motion, he snatched the book from the floor and hurled it at Billy's head. Billy sprang back from the doorway, deeply frightened, not so much *of* him as with him. Both of them stood panting on either side of the doorway, and then Billy went back to his own room.

Lawrence pretended to be totally unconcerned about such flare-ups, which occurred several times in the late winter. He eventually allowed Billy to re-establish a civil relationship with him; *After all,* Lawrence reasoned, *he should be the one to make up, after the way he insulted me right in my own room. I never did like him,* he reflected with strengthening satisfaction, *no I never did.* Billy didn't matter to him; in September when he was so alone, Billy could have helped. But now; what good was Billy? He was no athlete, no star, he did not possess that unconcerned majesty, he was a person of no importance. And Billy, who was just finding out about kindness, looked regretfully elsewhere for friends.

Except for these explosions, Lawrence maintained his admirable outer imperviousness throughout the winter. He spent spring vacation in Virginia with his family. It was an uneventful two weeks except for a bitter little fight with Janine. "You're changed and I hate you," she cried at the end of it, and then indignantly, "Who do you think you are, anyhow? I hate you!"

He returned in the middle of April to find Devon transformed. He had forgotten that the bleak lanes and roads were beautiful when the earth turned once again toward the sun. Tiny leaves of callow green sprouted from the gray branches of the skeletal trees, and the living scents of the earth hung in the air. Windows which had been stuck closed with winter were opened to allow the promising air to circulate;

the steamy dryness of his little room drifted away; when he opened the single window and the door a tantalizing breeze whipped across his papers and note-books, fluttered the college pennants on his wall, and danced on to the other rooms where his housemates stirred restlessly.

Then, unexpectedly, he began to slip in his studies. For two successive French classes he appeared unprepared, and when called on to discuss the lesson, he fumbled. The others snickered behind their notebooks. But the boy sitting next to him, with whom he had had a relationship consisting only of "Excuse me," and "Hard assignment, wasn't it?", nudged him in the ribs as they were going out after the second class and exclaimed robustly, "Boy, did *you* stink today!" Lawrence was about to coin some cutting rejoinder when the boy grinned broadly. "You were really lousy," he added, punching him again. Lawrence tried and failed to keep from grinning back, and then muttered that Well, it was spring wasn't it.

That afternoon he went as usual to watch the varsity lacrosse team practice. His own intramural team was having a game that day and could have used even his unsteady stick, but he had wrangled a medical excuse. Varsity lacrosse was almost as meaningful for him as varsity baseball, and he didn't have to watch Captain Marvel there. So he sat alone on the empty bleachers and followed the practice shots intently, watching the careless skill of the players, marveling at the grand unawareness with which they played. *This is the best part of the day*, he thought, *this is wonderful*. He pondered the assumptions on which these athletes operated, that they would not miss the ball, that if they did they would catch it next time, that their teammates accepted them regardless, that there was a basic peace among them taken for granted. Lawrence could take nothing for granted; *yes, this is the best part of the day*, he told himself, and as he watched the skillful, confident boys warming to the game he saw only himself, he watched the others but he was seeing himself, doing all the skillful, impossible things.

He looked very pleased, *This is the best*, he thought, and despair flamed up in him.

He decided not to stay for the whole practice, and wandering back to the gym he met his own team coming out; Hey, Lawrence, get dressed, There's a game, Lawrence, C'mon, Stuart, Whathahelleryadoin? The one thing he had wanted to avoid that day was his own team. Lately he always seemed to be stumbling into the very situations he wanted fervently to avoid.

"Yeah," he called lamely to them, "but I got a . . ." *medical excuse?* An Olympian unable to take the field because of sniffles? It wouldn't do. "Yeah, okay, I was just . . . the varsity . . . I thought maybe if I watched them . . ." Shouting complicated explanations was impossible, "you know," he yelled even though they were moving away, not listening, "I thought I might learn something."

"Forget the varsity, Varsity," one of them called over his shoulder. "The second-string Red midfield wants you."

. . . This then was the afternoon when Lawrence scored his first goal. He felt an odd looseness playing that day, the hot rays of the sun seemed to draw the rigidity out of his body, leaving his muscles and sinews free to function as they would. Something about the way he held his stick was different, he found himself in the right place at the right time; his teammates sensed the change and passed the ball to him, and in the last minutes of the game he made a fast instinctive turn around a burly Blue defenseman and scored the winning goal with a quick, sure shot.

It was a minor triumph which calmed his spirit for approximately seven minutes, until the invitation to the movies was issued and turned aside, until he crossed over the little arching bridge, observed the water where his heroic reflection had shone, and stepped onto the turf on the other side, the varsity field. By the time they reached the gym it was Law-

rence the unrecognized Olympian again, Lawrence the
unknown and unloved.

After his shower he dressed and went, as he so often
did, into the trophy room for a pacifying moment of
dreaming. He knew the inscription and most of the
names on the Fullerton Cup by heart, and in the
space below 1951—Robert Graves Hartshorne, he
would visualize 1952—Charles Taylor Morrell, for un-
questionably the cup would be Marvel's this year. And
the list should go on and on, with one celebrated name
after another (even perhaps 1954—Lawrence Bates
Stuart); but here reality always intervened. The fact,
the shocking fact was that the front plate of the cup
was almost filled, after Marvel's name had been inscribed the list would reach the little silver relief
statues around the base—the old-fashioned football
player looking slim and inadequate, the pompous baseball player with his squarely planted little cap, and
the others—there would be no more room. Nor was
there any space to start a second list, since all the remaining circumference of the cup was devoted to an
etched allegorical representation of the flame of
knowledge passing from hand to hand through the
ages, until it found its way into a device at the top, a
coat-of-arms of birds and Latin and moons which was
the seal of Devon.

Always a little amazed at this finiteness of the cup,
Lawrence backed thoughtfully away from it. Wasn't
this the core of everything, didn't it sum up, absorb,
glorify everything at Devon? And still, the cup would
be full this year. One of these days it would be moved
to a case along the walls with the other old trophies
which had once reigned in the niche, it would be hon-
orably, obscurely retired. In his imagination the heroic
list stretched back over cup after cup, into the past,
and forward, upon cups not yet conceived, into the
future. It was odd, he thought, all these great names
fading into the past, getting less important every year,
until finally they must just go out, like the last burned
out ember in a fire. It was sad of course, but well,
there was something almost *monotonous* about it.

Lawrence squirmed. He had never thought about time's passage before. It made him feel better to realize it now, to see that the circle of the years changed things; it wasn't all up to him personally.

Puzzled, he gazed around this chilly and damp chamber which had seemed so cool and serene in February, untouched by the bone-chilling winds outside or the rasping steam in the other rooms of the school.

But now it was April, and Lawrence felt and saw April everywhere. This room isn't a chapel at all, he thought with a passing wave of indignation, it's a crypt.

Then, right there in the trophy room, he yawned, comfortably. And stretching his legs, to get a feeling of cramp out of them, he strode contentedly toward the door, through which the sunlight poured, and as he stepped into it he felt its warmth on his shoulders. It was going to be a good summer.

He never knew that he was right in this, because Lawrence drowned that night, by the purest accident, in the river which winds between the playing fields. Bead and Bruce tried to save him; the water was very cold and black and the night moonless. They eventually found him, doubled over among some rushes. He had not cried out when the cramp convulsed him, so they did not know where to begin searching and after they found him, it was a hard, clumsy job getting him to shore. They tried artificial respiration at first, and then becoming very frightened, started for help. But then Bruce thought again and came back to try to revive him while Bead ran to the gym, completely disrupting the movie in his frantic search for a master.

There was a conference two days later, attended by the headmaster, the dean, Mr. Kuzak from Lawrence's house, Bruce and Bead. The boys explained that it had been just a little lark; students always swam in the river in the spring, and although they usually waited until it was warmer, they had decided in the Butt Room Saturday night to have the first swim of the season while the rest of the school was at the movie.

Bruce and Bead had planned it alone, but Lawrence had been there, very enthusiastic to go to the movie. Then when he heard they were going swimming, that had become the one thing he wanted to do.

"You know, sir," Bruce explained earnestly to the dean, "he was a good swimmer, and he wanted to go so much."

"Yeah," Bead confirmed this eagerly, "we didn't ask him to go, did we, Bruce?"

"No, he just asked if he could and we said yes."

Bead set his face maturely, "He wasn't a very good friend of ours, but he just wanted to go. So we said okay, but it wasn't like we planned it together. I didn't know him very well, did you, Bruce?"

"No, I didn't either."

Mr. Kuzak studied the backs of his hands, and the headmaster asked, "Who were his close friends?"

"I don't know," Bead answered.

"The fellows in his house, I guess," said Bruce. Everyone looked at Mr. Kuzak, who thought of several perfunctory ways of confirming this, but knowing it was not true, he was unable to say anything. It is easy to write, "Lawrence Stuart is beginning to find himself" on a report to the dean, when Stuart was alive and could be heard trudging up the stairs every day; undoubtedly he *would* have found himself. But now the boy was dead, Mr. Kuzak had seen his body, had telephoned his parents; he said nothing.

Irritated, the headmaster leaned out of his throne-like chair. "He *had* close friends?" he persisted.

Still Mr. Kuzak could not speak.

"Well," the dean broke the uneasy silence, his kind, mournful eyes studying the two boys, "Well how did he, was he—" his fingers searched the lines in his forehead, "he enjoyed it, did he?" The dean's face reddened, he indulged in his chronic cough for several seconds. "He seemed lively? I mean did he act . . . happy, before, before this cramp seized him?"

"Oh sure!" Bead exclaimed. "Yes, yes he did," Bruce said at the same time.

"When we first got there," Bruce continued, "he

got up on the bridge. Bead and I just slipped into the water from the bank, it was awfully cold."

"I never was in such cold water," Bead agreed.

"But Stuart got up on the bridge and stood there a minute."

"Then he dove," said Bead.

"Dived," someone corrected abstractly.

"It was a real dive," Bruce added thoughtfully. "He did a beautiful dive."

It had been like the free curve of powerful wings. Lawrence had cut the water almost soundlessly, and then burst up again a moment later, breaking a foaming silver circle on the black surface. Then he twisted over on his back and sank out of sight.

"I believe he enjoyed the water," said Mr. Kuzak quietly.

"Yeah," Bead agreed, "he liked it a lot, I think. That was the one thing he did like. He was good in the water."

"I don't think he cared," Bruce remarked suddenly.

The headmaster straightened sharply. "What do you mean?" Bruce's thoughts doubled over this instinctive statement, to censor it or deny it, but then because this was death and the first he had ever really encountered, he persisted. "I mean in the dive, he just seemed to trust everything, all of a sudden. He looked different, standing up there on the bridge."

"Happy?" asked the dean in a very low voice.

"Something like that. He wasn't scared, I know that."

The conference ended shortly afterward, with everyone agreed that it had been a wholly accidental death. A photograph of Lawrence in his swimming suit, taken when he made the junior varsity team, was enlarged, framed, and hung on the wall of the gym among pictures of athletic teams. He stood very straight in the picture and his young eyes looked directly at the camera.

But the season moved on; that summer was the most beautiful and fruitful anyone could remember at Devon. Blossoms scented the air and hung over the river winding quietly through the playing fields. And the earth, turned full toward the sun, brought forth its annual harvest.

The Scarlet Letter

BY JEAN STAFFORD

I KNEW from the beginning that Virgil Meade was crazy, but I didn't know he was a crook until it was too late and he had got me into a fine how-do-you-do that might have altered the whole course of my life. I mean I might have killed him and either gone to the gallows or spent the rest of my natural days in the pen.

Virgil unofficially became my fellow when he put a big valentine in the box for me. At first I was sorely affronted because it was a very insulting comic one he had made himself—when you opened it up, there was the outline of a huge foot on each page and underneath it said: "All policemen have big feet but Emily Vanderpool's got them beat." Moreover, he had signed it so there would be no doubt in my mind who was trying to hurt my feelings. I couldn't decide whether to write him a poison pen letter beginning "Dear (oh yeah?) Four-Eyes" or to beat him on the head with an Indian club. But then I discovered that he had written "s.w.a.k." on the back of the envelope and I knew what that stood for because my sister Stella, who was popular and was therefore up on codes and slang, had told me: "Sealed With a Kiss." Ordinarily such mushiness would have made me go ahead and write the letter or take out after him with the Indian club; but it so happened that at that particular time I didn't have a friend to my name, having fought with everyone I knew, and the painful truth was that Virgil's valentine was positively the only one I got that year except for a dinky little paper-doily thing, all bumpy with homemade paste, from my baby sister, Tess. And besides being all alone in the world, I was a good deal impressed by Virgil because he was as clever as a monkey on the parallel bars (the way he skinned the cat was *something*), and I had heard that at the age of eleven he already had a wisdom tooth, a rumor that seemed somehow the more likely because his father was a dentist. And so, on second thought, although he had insulted me and although he wore glasses (a stigma far more damning than the biggest clodhoppers in the world), I decided that he was better than nobody and I looked across the room at him. He was staring moodily out the window at the icicles, cracking his knuckles to the tune of "Shave and a haircut." To attract his attention I cracked mine in harmony, and he turned around and smiled at me. He had a nice smile, rather crooked and wry, and I liked his pert pug nose and the way his shiny black hair came to a neat widow's peak in the exact middle of his forehead.

We kept up our antiphony for about a minute and then Miss Holderness heard us and looked up from the valentine box she had been grubbing in. Her snappish brown eyes went darting around the room as, in her ever irascible voice, she cried: "Valentine's Day or no Valentine's Day, I decidedly will not tolerate any levity in this class. Who is making that barbarous noise?" She pushed up the paper cuffs that protected the sleeves of her tan challis dress and glared. There was one of those weighty, stifling silences in which everyone held his breath, everyone feeling accused and everyone feeling guilty. Finally, unable to single out any faces that looked more blameworthy than any others, she had to give up with the threat: "If there is ever again any knuckle-cracking in this class, the miscreant will go straight to Mr. Colby for his or her punishment. I have reiterated ad infinitum that levity is out of place in the sixth grade." (Miss Holderness abhorred children and she loved hard words. Once, after making me sing a scale by myself, she put her fingers in her ears and she said: "I have never heard such cacophony. Try it again, Emily, and this time endeavor not to agonize my Eustachian tube." To get even with her I read the dictionary that night and the next day asked her what "palimpsest" meant, but she outsmarted me by congratulating me on my intellectual curiosity and asking me to go to the Unabridged and read the definition out loud to the class. Everyone, including Miss Holderness, was baffled.) Virgil and I looked at each other again and grinned, and when Miss Holderness had bent her head once more to the valentine box he stuck out his tongue and thumbed his nose. This demoralized everybody in his immediate vicinity and a general giggle began like a gale. Luckily, all the valentines had been handed out and the bell rang and Miss Holderness dismissed us with a look of hatred. A humorist, especially an anti-teacher one, enjoys great prestige in grammar school, and the more I thought about it, the more I was sure I would realize considerable benefit in being associated with Virgil. My own status was at present so low, by reason of my many quarrels, that I could not possibly elevate it by myself and very quickly I began to look on Virgil as the savior who would raise me from my ignominy. Little did I dream that that wily boy had a long-range plan to ruin me.

As we were putting on our galoshes, Virgil asked if he could walk me home, thereby proving that his intentions were serious. I shrugged my shoulders and said: "Suit yourself. It's a free country." I may have sounded nonchalant, but actually I was already afire with that puzzling, unnamable feeling that had preceded each of my betrothals since the age of five (I was a roughneck, fond of Indian wrestling and addicted to swearing, but I was vulnerable to love and the lacunae between my romances were melancholy); my throat and eyes were hot, my stomach was uneasy, my brains ticktocked like an Ingersoll and some of my bones felt as if they were coming loose. As we were leaving the schoolyard, a two-legged rat, a former friend of mine—in fact, he was Virgil's predecessor, with whom once upon a time I had planned to grow old gracefully—Dicky Scott, saw us and yelled: "Red and yella, kiss your fella! You'll be sorry, Specs! Vanderloop-the-loop's a dizzy old doughhead!" Virgil put his books and his lunch box down on the stone wall and before you could say "Knife" he had made a good hard snowball and caught Dicky on the chin, surprising him so that he just stood there gaping and making no attempt to retaliate. Several other children who had witnessed the episode called, "Atta-boy, Meade!" and "You tell 'em, partner!" Nobody had anything against Dicky—it was simply that in our savage society it was de rigueur to applaud whoever cast the first stone. I was gratified that my honor had been so swiftly and brilliantly defended and I seemed to sense that my stock was going up among the spectators. Indeed, Ruby Miller, who had not spoken to me for two weeks after an altercation over the ownership of a roller-skate key (it belonged to her but I was too proud to admit it when I found that out) came up and said: "Will you come to my birthday party on the twenty-first of July? I'm going to wear silk stockings."

Virgil and I walked home in total silence. Sometimes, in unspoken agreement, we walked stiff-legged; sometimes we left the cleared path and scuffed through the snow up to our knees. In the last block we broad-jumped from crack to crack in the sidewalk. Nobody was home at my house and I was glad of that because I wanted our first interview to be conducted without any interference from Mother (who had some crazy idea that kids liked to be asked such questions as "Have your folks taken up the new contract bridge that's all the rage?" or "What does your mother think about taking off the interurban and running buses to Denver?") or from Jack and Stella, who loved to tease me about my suitors. I made some sandwiches for Virgil and me of peanut butter and piccalilli and mayonnaise and Virgil said it was better than eating a fried chicken dinner. I told him to go on —this was the standard after-school sandwich in every house in Adams I'd ever been in—but he said he'd never eaten one before and he asked if he could have another. "Pardon me for living, girl, but can I have seconds?" He used this expression, "Pardon me for living," to precede almost everything he said, and although I didn't know exactly what it meant, it sounded sporty and I filed it away to spring on my family as soon as I could. When we had eaten we went into the living room and Virgil told me some riddles and jokes he had learned from his father, who was in great demand as the end man for minstrel shows at the B.P.O.E. One riddle was "What's black and white and red all over?" and the answer was *not* "A newspaper" but "A blushing zebra." Another was "Why is the Statue of Liberty's hand eleven inches long?" The answer was that if it were twelve inches it would be a foot. He taught me several Mr. Tambo–Mr. Bones dialogues and we decided that when it got warmer we would put on a show in his father's garage. His father, he said, had the latest thing in make-up kits—grease paint, false noses, funny whiskers.

Then we talked about what we were going to do when we grew up; it was a romantic coincidence that I was going to be an organist in a movie house and Virgil was going to be an usher, and we both planned to follow our calling in a big city, Omaha, perhaps, or Chicago. Virgil and I had a great deal in common; we both walked in our sleep and had often waked up just before we fell out of the window or down the stairs; both of us loved puzzles and card games and the two things in the world we really detested were Sunday school (Virgil said in so many words that he didn't believe in God) and geography homework.

"Down with the blankety-blank principal exports of the Malay Archipelago," said this articulate and forthright boy. "Gutta-percha—don't make me laugh."

"Tell the class all you know about the Hottentots," I said, imitating Miss Holderness, and Virgil got up and stood on his head, putting his feet against the wall. Upside down he said: "The Hottentots eat gutta-percha out of gutta-percha nose bags and they teach their grandmothers how to suck eggs."

Reddie, the dog, came padding in and looked at Virgil for a long time and then he yawned and padded out again. After that, Muff, the cat, came in to give Virgil the once-over. Virgil righted himself and waved his hands madly at Muff, who walked out of the room slowly, twitching her tail with disgust. Virgil said, "If there's one thing I can't stand it's to have an animal rubberneck at me. Especially cows. Pardon me for living, if a cow rubbernecks at me, I sock it right on the snoot," and he went on to tell me how he showed who was boss when he went to visit at his uncle's ranch on the western slope. There was a cow named Hildy that he had pasted in the beezer more than once and there was also a gawking billy goat that he had given a good lesson to. I was thrilled to think of this brave gladiator striding through pastures walloping cows that gave him the eye and when he said, "I'm about the only man in this town that can make those mangy old burros of Mr. Hodge's turn off their headlights," I was bowled over with admiration and I exclaimed, "Boy, you're the only man I ever heard of that can do it." Virgil promised that some day soon he would take me up to Mr. Hodge's ratty shack on the mesa and show me how he could make the little donkeys "see stars instead of yours truly." The fact was that I dearly loved those little animals, Pearl and Princess, and whenever Jack and I got a quarter saved up we hired them from Mr. Hodge and rode them all over town. And here, out of blinding rapture, I was accepting an invitation to watch Virgil mistreat them.

He made a general survey of the living room. He picked the Bible up off the library table and said, "Phooey," and then he began to examine the Civil War saber that had belonged to a bounty-jumping relative on my mother's side. He unsheathed it and hefted it and he said thoughtfully: "This may come in handy sometime."

After a pause he said: "Pardon me for living, girl, can I have another one of those keen sandwiches?" While he ate it Reddie came out to the kitchen to watch him with his big heartbroken hungry eyes and Virgil slapped him on the nose. "You heard me, you good-for-nothing scalawag," he said. "Don't you look at me and my sandwich with your googly-googly eyes." Reddie, the meekest thing in the world, looked as if he were going to cry, and when I, disloyal to my nice old dog because I was in love with this blood-thirsty swashbuckler, laughed, he cringed and slunk out of the room, and for the rest of the afternoon he lay under the china closet in the dining room with his head between his paws.

Virgil pardoned himself for living again and again asked for a sandwich. When he was finally satisfied and we went back to the living room he told me a sad story that explained why he was so hungry. He said that at home they had nothing to eat but dough-nuts. His mother made about a million of them on Sunday, enough to last a week, and every day they had doughnuts with maple sirup for breakfast. These she called "doughnut waffles"; for supper she put ketchup on them and called them "doughnut meat-balls" or "doughnut roast." "Doughnut surprise" had canned salmon and peas in the doughnut hole and it was awful. At one of the sanitariums in our town the food was all made of cereal; the cranky old valetudi-narians ate things like "Grape Nut cutlet" and "Corn Flake loaf," a bill of fare that never ceased to amaze and sadden my mother, who occasionally had lunch there with a friend of my grandmother's. So I got the idea that Mrs. Meade was some sort of invalid and I thought it was cruelly unfair that everybody in her family willy-nilly had to follow her diet. But after a while I realized that Virgil was only telling lies be-cause he went on to say that the reason they only had doughnuts was that his mother had bats in the belfry and spent all her time, when she should have been cooking for her growing children, collecting cold cream jars in the alleys and on the dump. She caught the bats in her belfry in the cold cream jars, screwed the lids down tight and sent them by post to her nutty twin sister in Boise who was named Aunt Dandelion. Aunt Dandelion! Did he really think I was dumb enough to believe a name like that?

This is what I mean about Virgil being crazy. One time he told me that he had been kidnaped by a runaway convict from Canon City named Ben the Red Beard. The desperado, who had murdered hundreds and permanently crippled many more with his six-shooter, handcuffed Virgil and took him up to a shack in the mountains and kept him there for three days. On the third night, after the man was asleep, Virgil managed to crawl over to the grocery supplies and he ate three big onions; then he crawled back to the cot where Ben the Red Beard was snoring away and breathed into his face until the kidnaper, undone by the fumes, took off the handcuffs and Virgil was free. He had walked all the way home in the dark, a distance of twenty-two miles, and it was seventeen below zero. When I asked him why his family hadn't sent out a posse for him, he said: "I go away for three or four days at a time by myself without telling them and they don't mind—I mean, if they did mind, I'd tell them where to get off. I go deer hunting, you see. Last year, I got an eight-point buck up by the glacier but I gave it away to some bootleggers I know. And now and then I hop a rattler and go down to Denver and hang around Larimer Street playing pool for two or three days."

Virgil left long before anyone came home, but there were traces of him everywhere. When he had stood on his head he had left two precise footprints on the white wall; his voracity had done away with most of the bread and all of the peanut butter; Reddie was still grieving and Mother, thinking he was sick, wanted to call the vet. Naturally I couldn't take the blame for all these things and had to let the cat out of the bag. When I told Mother why Reddie was so woebegone, she was at first too shocked to speak and then she said: "Emily, no good will ever come of this friendship, you mark my words." Would that I had! I tried to make up with Reddie but Jack snarled, "You stay away from him," and Stella, weeping, implored Mother to send me away, anywhere, so that she would never again have to lay eyes on a dastardly tormentor of man's best friend.

I was chastened, but I had no intention of giving up Virgil and thereafter we had our sandwiches at his house. They were usually made of peanut butter, mayonnaise and piccalilli—I never saw a single doughnut in his house and the smells in his mother's kitchen were perfectly delicious. I had been right about one thing: though my family might deplore my new alliance, the other kids looked on it with envy because Virgil and I were always whispering and passing notes in school and we refused to play or even talk with anyone else. Dicky Scott one day offered me an arrowhead and I haughtily refused—I might have accepted it but I happened to know, because Dicky himself had one time unwisely told me, that it was spurious.

Virgil and I were together every afternoon except on ballet day. Sometimes we coasted and sometimes we made lists (of kinds of automobiles, of three-letter words, of the movies we had seen), but usually we just sat in his father's den and talked. I loved this dark and crowded room that smelled of cigars and furniture polish, and I wished that my own father had a room of his own. The walls were hung with all sorts of documents in frames, diplomas, certificates of membership in dental and social and religious societies; there was a serape with a bird and a snake on it; there was a tomahawk, a collection of minerals, an Indian headdress that Virgil said had once belonged to King Philip. On the roll-top desk, whose pigeonholes were so stuffed that nothing could ever be inserted in any of them, there was an enormous typewriter that had eight banks, three for the upper-case letters, three for the lower and two for the characters. When we used it, as we often did (wrote our names, wrote "Down with Miss Holderness"), it sounded like a small tractor and its bell was like one on a trolley car. Here, seated in leather armchairs, we were continually eyed by Virgil's dog, a His Master's Voice dog, who lay on a deerskin rug. We discussed our many projects. For one thing, we planned to make a trip in the summer with a wagon and horses up to a mine where Virgil knew that a lot of pieces of eight were buried; this involved making lists of what we would take and we wrote out a long order to Montgomery Ward— Virgil said the money would turn up somehow. Then there was the minstrel show we were going to put on and we had to rehearse our acts.

More immediately, though, what we talked about was a plan we had to draw up a petition against geography homework, which was really ruining our lives and the lives of everybody else in the sixth grade. At least three thousand years ago Miss Holderness had gone around the world with some other old maids and she never stopped bragging about rice paddies and rickshas and the Yangtze and Big Ben. She was forever passing around pale brown picture post cards that showed camels, Norwegian fisheries and the Victoria and Albert Museum; she showed us a little bottle with water from the Jordan and an ordinary pebble she had picked up in the neighborhood of the Taj Mahal. Every blessed night of the world we had to get something by heart—the chief rivers of Asia, the capitals of the Isles of Greece, European mountain ranges, famous monuments in Rome—and the next day she would either give us a paper test or would single out some poor kid to recite, and it seemed to Virgil and me that the poor kid was always one of us. We had to make relief maps with salt and flour and each Friday afternoon during the last period, when we were all wild with fidgets, she made us draw a map of the United States from memory; to this day I don't know whether Delaware is on the left-hand side of Maryland or the right, and I can never find room for Vermont. Talk about a one-track mind.

One Friday afternoon she told us that by Monday we would have to know all the counties of England, and Virgil and I decided that this was the limit and the time had come for us to act. I had intended to depart from custom that afternoon and go straight home, because that morning at Assembly I had won a school letter for collateral reading and I wanted to sew it on the sleeve of my middy right away, but Virgil said: "Pardon me for living, girl, haven't you got any class spirit? Do you know that this geography junk may keep us in the sixth grade for eighty-nine years?" He said we had no time to lose, that everybody was now so mad at Holderness (hadn't I heard the whole room groan?) that we'd have no trouble getting signatures for our petition. We must draw it up this afternoon and then spend tomorrow going from door to door getting people to sign. "In *ink*," said Virgil. "This has gotta be official with no ifs and buts about it." And so, ever his slave, I went along home with him.

I want to say something about that afternoon that isn't related to the Mutiny of the Sixth Grade of Carlyle Hill but will show you the kind of looniness Virgil was capable of. His mother wasn't home that day so Virgil made the sandwiches. He couldn't find the peanut butter but he said for me not to look and he would make a surprise. I'll say he made a surprise. He made those sandwiches of Campbell's vegetable soup and I'm not kidding. I was eating this stuff and I couldn't tell for the life of me what it was; it didn't taste bad but it *felt* funny, so I surreptitiously turned my back and lifted up the top slice of bread and there I saw a lima bean. And then I saw the empty can on the drainboard.

After the soup sandwiches and after one game of Shasta Sam, we got down to work in the den. Among Dr. Meade's framed testimonials there was a bounty land grant awarded to Virgil's Great-Uncle Harry, who had fought at Murfreesboro. It was signed by Abraham Lincoln, and Virgil, taking it down and handing it to me, said it was worth several million

dollars. (If all the things in the Meades' house had
had the value Virgil assigned to them, Dr. Meade
could have retired and bought the Teapot Dome.) We
would use it, said Virgil, as the model for our petition because it had a high and mighty tone and high
and mighty was what we were going to be from now
on. Virgil typed while I dictated, paraphrasing the
land grant. It was uphill work because every key
stuck and the *s* wouldn't budge at all so that had to
be filled in later with ink. But when we were finished
we were pleased with the results, although there were
mistakes abounding. The petition (more properly, the
declaration) read:

> HTE SIXTH GRADEO%F CRaLYLE HILL
> GRADE SCHOOL OF ADAMS
> TO?ALLT
> TO ALL TI WHOM THESE PRESENTS SHALL
> COME ¼ GREETING WHEREAS, in persuance
> of the act of Ggeography Ha Enemys, approved
> March 2, 1926, entitled aN Act to Stop Geography
> Homewoork, the undersigned people will not do any
> more Geograph HomeWork because it is not fair to
> give t so much of it.

We left a space for the signatures and then:

> NOW NOW YE, that there is ther3fore granted by
> the Surveyor Genersl of this class unto the said un-
> dersigned the privelege tto have and to hold, of NO
> MORE Geography HOMEWORK AND TO their
> heirs the privelege above described with the apuur-
> tenances therefo.
> WHEREOF I,   , have caused these letters
> to be made patent and affixed my signature thereto.

Abraham Lincoln's name was after the "WHEREOF I"
and we debated what to write there. We thought it
would look wrong to say "WHEREOF WE" and sign
both our names and at last Virgil gallantly said that
my name should be there because I now had a school

letter and this gave me a status he didn't have. He
said I should be the one, too, to hand it to Miss Holderness and he suggested that on Monday morning I
carry Mother's Civil War saber to school, not to in-
timidate Miss Holderness but to carry out the motif
of the Civil War. He rather regretfully rejected King
Philip's headdress as an anachronism.

He said: "Boy, oh, boy, can I see old Prune Face
when you march into the room with the sword and
say, 'Madam, allow me to present these presents,' and
you hand her this!"

A flicker of trepidation entered my infatuated mind
and I said: "What if she sends me to Mr. Colby and
I get expelled?"

"She'd have to send the whole class—everybody's
name will be there. Pardon me for living, girl, you're
not by any chance getting cold feet? Because if you
are—well, you know how I feel about cowards. I
wouldn't be seen at a dogfight with a coward."

I blushed and hastily said that of course I wasn't
getting cold feet, what was there to get cold feet about
—as he had said, if anybody had to go to Mr. Colby,
we'd all have to go. Anyhow, Holderness wouldn't
have any right to punish us since we were protected
by freedom of speech. Reassured that I was stout-
hearted, Virgil smiled his crooked smile and began to
tinker with the petition, putting in the absent *s*'s and
filling in the *o*'s. When he had finished he handed me
the scratchy pen and said: "Here, put your John
Hancock here on the dotted line." When I had signed
—the pen went through the paper a couple of times
and a big blob of ink floated like a rain cloud over
my surname—I was both scared and proud and had a
stomach sensation that was half-pleasant and half-
terrible. I was by no means sure that freedom of
speech would cover our action; I was by no means
sure that a petition of this sort was not against the
law, and to distract my thoughts from the possible
consequences of our daring I took my red felt C out
of my book bag and held it up to my sleeve.

Virgil said: "Listen, Emily, you know what? Why

don't you sew it on someplace else? Someplace different? So you'll be different from the common herd?"

"Like on my back?" I asked. "You mean like an athlete?"

"No, I was thinking of like on your sock."

"My *sock*!" I yelled. "Have you gone cuckoo?" But I rather liked the idea and I placed the letter experimentally on the outside of my right leg about in the middle of my shank. The bright red looked very striking against my navy blue knee-length sock, sort of like a cattle brand.

"Higher," said Virgil critically. "Yeah, right there. Hey, that's the pig's wings."

"Well, I don' know . . ." I began doubtfully, for on reconsideration it seemed to me that the letter would be more conspicuous on my sleeve. But Virgil said, "I double dare you," and that, of course, was that: I went home and blanket-stitched the scarlet letter on my sock. That evening when I went into the dining room and my family saw what I had done, they all began to fuss at me. My mother, who was active in the P.T.A., said: "Why, Emily, do you think that's a nice thing to do when Miss Holderness was so nice to give you that letter?"

"Miss Holderness was so nice! What did that dopey old goop have to do with it?" I demanded. "I suppose she read all those books and wrote all those reports. I'll have you know I *earned* this letter. And anyhow the *school* gave it to me."

"Well, then, the school was nice," said Mother, missing the point as usual. "Oh, Emily, why must you forever and a day be so contrary?"

"Because she's a scurvy rapscallion black sheep," said Jack, who had barely spoken to me since Virgil had upset Reddie.

"Baa, baa, black sheep, Emily's a black sheep," chanted copycat Tess and began to bubble her milk.

"Shut up, you little wart hog," I said to her and she did, terrified.

"Miss Holderness is not a dopey old goop," said Stella, who was sanctimonious and stood up for authority of all kinds. "She's a lady which is something you're never going to be in a thousand million years."

"Lady! Who wants to be a *lady?*" I said. "You make me sick." I made a sound of intense nausea and then I said: "Hasten, Jason, bring the basin. Ulp! Too late! Bring the mop!"

My father put down his napkin and faced me with his chin outthrust. "Now you listen to me, Emily Vanderpool. I've had just about enough of your shenanigans. I will not have bad language at my supper table and I will not have wrangling, do you hear me? I'm a hard-working man and when I come home at night, I'm tired and I want peace and quiet instead of this eternal confounded trouble you're always stirring up."

The unfairness of his attack brought tears to my eyes. Had anyone in the history of the world ever been so lamentably misunderstood? My voice was quivery as I said: "I didn't start it. Everybody started picking on *me* about my own personal property, damn it to hell!"

"What did I say about bad language?" he shouted, rising menacingly from his chair.

The devil at that moment made a conquest of my tongue and, blue in the face with fury, my eyes screwed shut, my fists clenched, I delivered a male-diction in the roughest billingsgate imaginable, vili-fying everyone at the table, all the teachers at Carlyle Hill, my uncles and aunts and cousins, my father's best friend, Judge Bay. The reaction was the same as it always was to one of my tantrums: appalled, fasci-nated, dead silence. When I was finished Jack, awed, said: "Yippy-ki-yi! That was a humdinger of a one!" I threw my glass of water in his face and stamped out of the room.

That was the last that was said at home about my school letter and when Stella came into the room we shared, she was at pains not to cross the chalk line I had drawn down the middle of the floor and not to speak to me: if she had uttered one word, on any sub-ject whatsoever, I would have beaten the hide off her.

The next day a blizzard somewhat hampered Virgil and me in our house-to-house canvass. Most people were at home because the wind made it uncomfortable coasting weather, and though this meant that they were easy to find (and so bored that they were delighted to see us), it also meant that there were a lot of nosy mothers around, asking questions and trying to distract us from our mission by inviting us to make popcorn or taffy. We had very little respect for the intelligence of these snoops, but we didn't want to run the risk of having some one of them call up Miss Holderness and spill the beans, and so we had to dally in a number of houses and pretend we had just come to pay a social call. We got stuck in Valerie Bemis' house for nearly an hour while her mother showed us views of Yellowstone and the Grand Canyon through a stereopticon.

To our considerable surprise and disappointment, we found that several of our classmates were partisans of Miss Holderness' (Estelle Powell, for instance, said she loved our teacher because she smelled so wonderful) and we found, furthermore, that the phobia for geography homework was not, after all, universal. Indeed, six or seven stick-in-the-muds said they liked it better than anything else and they refused to sign the petition. Ruby Miller admitted that she agreed with us, but she had already learned the English counties and didn't want them to go to waste, so she too refused to sign. This schism disturbed us, but all the same, at the end of the day, we had a majority of seventeen names. It was dark by the time we left the last house and the street lights had come on. Under a light beside a mailbox we paused in the whirling snow and Virgil solemnly put the petition in a long envelope, solemnly handed it to me and solemnly said: "Pardon me for living, girl, but this will probably get us into the Hall of Fame. Good luck." And with this he started off in the direction of his house, his dramatic shadow long and lean beside him.

When the sixth grade got into line on Monday morning there was an undercurrent of great excite-

ment and everybody was looking at me: there were
gasps from those who caught sight of the honor badge
on my leg, there were uneasy whispers about my Civil
War saber, which was imperfectly hidden under my
coat. Someone murmured in my ear, "Scratch out my
name, Emily, please?" and someone else said: "Looky,
if you're going to kill her, I don't want to have anything to do with it." I glared fiercely but I didn't
feel fierce, I felt foolish and scared because Virgil
Meade was nowhere to be seen.

The soft exclamations of incredulity and fear continued as we marched into the building and hung up
our wraps, and even after we had said, "Good morning, Miss Holderness," and had sat down there was
still a faint buzzing and thrumming like noises in the
grass on a summer day.

"Quiet, please!" said Miss Holderness and clapped
her hands smartly. "What is the meaning of this deaf-
ening pandemonium?"

There was immediate silence and then Johnny
Thatcher, who had not signed the petition, held up
his hand and giggled and said: "Emily has something
to show you, teacher."

"I see Emily's sword," said Miss Holderness. I had
tried to put it under my desk but it stuck out into the
aisles on each side. "And I think we will simply ignore
it. We do not know why she brought it to school and
we do not care to know."

Johnny Thatcher said: "No, I don't mean that.
She's got something else to show you. Something
about geography homework."

"Very well, Emily," said the teacher, snapping her
fingers and snapping her eyes. "Show me what it is.
We cannot spend the entire day on the subject of
Emily Vanderpool's tricks to attract attention to herself. Come along, Emily, quickly, quickly!"

"I haven't got anything," I stammered.

"You have too," said Johnny.

Everyone began to babble at once and Miss Holderness angrily rapped her desk with her ruler. "I have a
good mind to punish everyone in this class," she said.

"Emily, I want you to show me whatever this is at once."

Reluctant, furious, I stumbled up to the desk and put the petition down in front of her. She gave me a black look and then she opened the envelope; as she read, moving her lips, her color rose until she looked like an apple.

"So!" she cried. "So Miss Emily Vanderpool is now known as 'the surveyor-general of this class.' I was not aware that elections had been held and she had been voted into office."

Everyone tittered.

"I . . ." I began, but Miss Holderness held up her hand for silence.

"Now let me see," she said and began checking the names on the petition against those in the class book. There was a pause and every heart beat wildly. Then she said, "Ruby, Estelle, Homer, Johnny, Marjorie and Virgil—these are the children who are still loyal to Carlyle Hill Grade School and have not kowtowed to this self-styled surveyor-general. Children, I congratulate you."

"Virgil!" I cried. "But Virgil . . ." Then, because I did not want to be a tattletale, even against that foxy fourflusher, I held my peace.

"What about Virgil?" asked Miss Holderness. "I am sorry that Virgil is absent today, for I would like him to know how deeply I appreciate his refusing to affix his signature to this outrageous scrap of paper. Shame on you, Emily Vanderpool, shame on you!"

She looked me up and down with revulsion as if I were a reptile or a skunk and suddenly she saw the school letter on my sock. She gaped, speechless, and then said: "Ruby, I shall leave you in charge of the class. Emily and I have some business to transact in Mr. Colby's office."

That was a long last mile I walked. I thought sadly and enviously of all the children behind the closed doors who would continue their lives of ease and re-

spectability while I was working on a mason gang at
the reform school. All my sensations were intense: the
smell of cedar shavings was stronger than ever and the
smell of wet Mackinaws and overshoes (overshoes are
made of gutta-percha, I thought sorrowfully, homesick for the principal exports of the Malay Archipelago), and the sounds of teachers' voices and the
thud of feet and balls in the gym below and the piping
squeals from the kindergarten room were like a loud
song of farewell to me. Miss Holderness' hand, grasp-
ing my arm, was a cruel metal claw.

Mr. Colby was an asthmatic old man with a purple-
veined nose and a sorrel toupee. He had very short
legs but he had strong, broad shoulders and sitting behind his magisterial desk he looked like a giant. His
two bluebell blue eyes were on quite different levels,
giving him a quizzical and half-amused look as if he
were trying to figure out a joke he didn't entirely
understand. He was playing with a sharp letter opener
when we came into his office, flicking the point with
his index finger as he made half-revolutions in his
swivel chair. He invited Miss Holderness to sit down
and with the letter opener indicated the place where I
was to stand, directly in front of his desk. Several
times in the course of my teacher's indignant recital
of my felonies he swiveled himself completely around
so that his back was to us and he coughed and wheezed
—it sounded like strangled laughter. When he leaned
over his desk to look at my shameful leg he had such
a seizure that he had to bury his face in his handker-
chief, and when he read the petition I thought he was
going to explode. After the case against me had been
stated, Mr. Colby told Miss Holderness to go back to
her class and said that he would deal with me himself.

"Now, Emily," he said when she was gone, "there
is no doubt about the gravity of your misdemeanors
. . . incidentally, why did you bring a sword to
school?"

"Well, it's a Civil War one and Vir . . . I mean it's a
Civil War one and since the petition was a Civil War
thing . . ."

"A Civil War thing? What sort of thing?"

"Just a thing. I don't know what you call it. But where my name is is really Abraham Lincoln's name."

He wheeled his chair around again and he wheezed for quite some time. "The name of Emily Vanderpool has been substituted for that of Honest Abe," he said at length. "The case grows stranger. I confess to a certain amount of confusion. I can't seem to see the tie-in with the sword, the petition and your putting your school letter on your stocking, a gesture tantamount, as Miss Holderness so aptly put it, to dragging the Star-Spangled Banner in the dirt. Can you help me out?"

Mr. Colby's voice, though firm, was kind and his funny eyes were sweet and though my legs were buckling and my heart thundered I longed to tell him the whole truth. But naturally I could not without involving Virgil and I said only, as mad murderers often do: "I don't know why I did it."

He picked up the petition again and this time I thought he was really going to fly apart. He threw back his head so far I thought his toupee would surely fall off and he coughed and wheezed and gurgled fearsomely. "You'll be the death of me!" he howled and I thought I really would be. He groped, blinded with tears, for a bottle of pills and a carafe of water, and when he had dosed himself and straightened his vest and put on a pair of severe spectacles he gave me a sober lecture on the value of geography and the sin of insubordination, the inadvisability of carrying arms, the folly of arrogating power, the extreme impropriety of wearing an honor badge on the leg. Finally he told me to go back to my room and apologize to Miss Holderness and then to go home for the rest of the day and explain to my mother exactly why I was in disgrace. When I had closed the door behind me I heard him having another attack and I knew that it would be the gallows for me if he died.

For the next two weeks I was in double dishonor. Miss Holderness made me stay after school every day and write lists of rivers and cities and principal ex-

ports. I had to go home immediately thereafter and
stay in my room with the door closed until suppertime.
Jack and Stella did not speak one word to me. During
those weeks I was not allowed to wear my letter even
in its proper place. The sixth grade got more geography homework than ever and consequently I was
sent to Coventry by all my classmates. I crept around
like a sick dog and wished I were dead.

At first the namby-pamby boobs in my grade took
Virgil's side against me even though they knew good
and well that I could have got him in Dutch too if I
had snitched. They all knew, of course, that he had
been just as responsible for the petition as I, but they
did not know that he had put me up to sewing the C
on my sock and it was this act of insolence to dear
old Carlyle Hill that they regarded as my cardinal
crime. For the two weeks of my quarantine Virgil
enjoyed an immense, ill-gotten popularity, and I heard,
with mixed feelings, that he was practically engaged
to Ruby Miller. I did not deign to recognize his existence.

And then, on the very day I was first allowed to
wear my letter, silly Virgil tipped his hand. Ruby
Miller told me during lunch hour. At morning recess
she and he had been swapping bird cards out of Arm
and Hammer Baking Soda boxes as I passed by. Ruby
saw that I was wearing my letter again and asked Virgil
why he thought I had done that awful thing. Ruby
said, "Who would *think* of doing a thing like that?"
and Virgil had said: "I'll tell you somebody who
wouldn't and that's Vanderloop-the-loop—she's too
dumb. *I* told her to sew it on her leg."

The news spread rapidly, whispered during Palmer
Method, written on notes in Current Events, and by
the end of the afternoon session I was in and Virgil
was out. People came up to me singly and in groups
to congratulate me on my nobility; some of them
shook my hand. I accepted their acclaim with a wan
and martyred smile, thanked them for their many in-
vitations to visit their houses but said that I had to go
home because I was reading the Bible.

I remained aloof only that one day and the next day plunged into a social whirl. Virgil, as it was fitting, was totally ostracized. In time I took pity on him; indeed, some months later, we again became boon companions, but I saw to it that he never hoodwinked me again: I ruled him with an iron glove and after he had made one slip he never made another.

The slip was this. We were walking home one day in the spring and he picked a leaf off a lilac bush. He said to me: "If you can divide this exactly in half, I'll give you a quarter." What could be easier than dividing a lilac leaf? The midrib is clear and the flesh is crisp, and I accomplished the feat in a second. "o.k., where's my quarter?" I said and Virgil, tearing one of the halves of the leaf in two, handed me a piece. "Here's your quarter," he said and doubled up with laughter. I simply looked at him and then I turned and walked away. He came running after me, begging for mercy, reminding me of all the good times we'd had together. I marched on for two blocks, ignoring him, but then, at a vacant lot, I stopped, climbed up on top of a boulder and told him to kneel on the ground. Then, like Moses on Mount Sinai, I laid down the law, and ever after that Virgil Meade was the most tractable boon companion I had.

The Valentine
By James Jones

JOHN SLADE had not meant for it to become such a big operation, such a production. But from the moment he had first stepped into Woolworth's with his mind made up and had gone up to the candy counter and picked out the box, that was what it seemed to become. And now, the last day before Valentine's Day, with Woolworth's ready to close in just a few minutes, everything couldn't have been worse.

In the first place, there were two other paper boys from the newsstand standing there at the candy counter. And the man behind the counter was a man he knew. He was sort of the assistant manager. He had squinchy eyes and liked to needle the kids. And the two other paper boys from the newsstand were both freshmen, while he was still only an eighth-grader. It couldn't have been a much worse situation to try and buy the box in.

And this time he couldn't go away and come back another time, as he had already done three other times during the past week when he had come in and found other people standing at the candy counter. Either he had to do it now or not do it. Unless he went somewhere else, like the drugstore, and he didn't want to do that, because he knew the box he wanted, had in fact picked it out as long as two weeks ago, and it was, for the money, which was $6.95, the best box in town—all hearts that interlocked with each other within the big heart that was the box itself, and with two small paper cupids in the center of the white paper lace in the middle of that striking, eye-stopping, deep,

deep red. A really beautiful box. And if he didn't take it now, after having promised himself that he would, he felt quite strongly that there would be no way out of having to face the fact that he was afraid and a liar to himself, and a coward.

It was the first time in his life that John Slade had ever really bought anything for a girl, and he wanted so bad for it to be right, as if he had done it a thousand times. Especially since the girl herself, whose lovely beautiful name was Margaret Simpson, didn't know anything about it at all yet, and wouldn't until he handed the box to her tomorrow. He wanted it to be a surprise. And he wanted it to be a secret. As far as that went, he was forced to admit, he didn't have nerve enough to do it any other way. Because he couldn't just go up to her and mention it. She might refuse. And now——

Some secret this would be! he thought. And he stood irresolute just inside the door in his corduroy, sheepskin-collared Mackinaw, despairing.

What did those guys have to be there for? And why did that sort of assistant manager have to be behind the counter? Any clerk in the store would have been better. Hell, he would have been better off if he'd gone ahead and bought it one of those other times when he'd chickened out. He didn't want it to be a big operation. But everybody made it that.

There wasn't any possibility of waiting those two guys out. They obviously weren't leaving, and there was less than five minutes left till closing. And he knew that Woolworth's weren't going to stay open one minute after five for any 13-year-old kid. Unless he could succeed in covering it up from the two big kids some way—and how could he do that with that loudmouth needler behind the counter?—it would mean he would take an awful lot of razzing at the newsstand for the next month or so.

The newsstand was a good place to work, the best of the several possible paper-carrying jobs in town, and it was not, in this town, at any rate, the kind of poor-people, low-class idea of a job that most people had of paper boys in a city, for instance. The boys who worked at the newsstand were a cross section of the whole town, from the very poorest, like Otis Cole, to the most well-off; one of the boys at the counter was a doctor's son and the other a lawyer's, and he himself was the son of a dentist. But that, just the same, did not mean they weren't capable of inflicting the most roasting kind of humiliating razzing, especially when it came to anything like girls. Sex was one thing, and it seemed that almost everybody talked about that, but when it came to girl friends and being in love! That was something else again, and you were liable to get yourself laughed and razzed right out of the back room of the newsstand in the predawn early mornings when everybody folded their papers before taking off. And if they found out about anybody buying a girl a great big heart-shaped box of candy for Valentine's Day!

In his case it would be even worse, since Margaret Simpson (gee, what a lovely, beautiful name that was) was not his girl friend and never had been, and had never had any dates with him (he had never had any dates with anyone, in fact). Margaret was known to have dated freshmen in high school and even a few sophomores this past year; but he was going to ask her for a date as soon as he gave her the box tomorrow. Still, nobody knew now that he had fallen in love with her. That would make terrific news at the newsstand, after tomorrow, and it wouldn't do him any good to deny it, although he would. It wouldn't even matter if the whole thing wasn't even true, for that matter, once the guys got the idea in their heads.

For a moment, as the seconds ticked agonizingly on toward five o'clock and the hanging moment of ultimate decision, John seriously considered the luxury of just abandoning the whole project, of just turning around and going off and forgetting the whole thing and just buying her a cheap little box someplace else. Nobody would even notice a small, cheap box. Just the idea of it was an enormous relief. But he knew he could never do it. Not after having exacted of himself a solemn, faithful promise that he would go through with it. He would never be able to trust his promises again. That was the very reason he had made himself promise. So he couldn't back out.

With a feeling of acute desolation, he took hold of himself mentally, so to speak, and placed both hands in the center of his own thin back and shoved himself slowly over to the counter as if he were shoving a friend on roller skates, and mumbled.

"What is it, boy? What is it? Speak up."

Louder, John said, "I said I want that six-ninety-five one there. How much is it?" His hand was in his pocket, nervously fingering his money, and he knew his mistake immediately and cursed himself for it. Old squinch-eye was staring down at him from across the counter with the beginning of his evil grin.

"How much is it!" the assistant manager said loudly, laughing. "You just told me yourself. It's six ninety-five. What do you mean how much is it?"

"I'll take it," John said nervously, fighting to keep his eyes looking straight at the squinchy ones. "Wrap it up." Down the counter he could see the two guys from the newsstand nudging each other.

"Yes, *sir*, Mr. Slade!" the Woolworth man grinned, his eyes squinching up even further. "Right *away*, sir!" He grinned down the counter at the other two guys. "Will there be anything else, sir?"

John tried to make it sound offhand, but he could tell his voice was shaky: "Nope. I guess that'll be all."

"Got yourself a new girl friend, hunh?" the assistant manager said loudly, as he began to wrap the box. "Man, you really must be stuck on her. Six ninety-five for a box of candy." He lowered his voice. "Want to tell me who she is?" he said slyly. The other two guys from the newsstand were sidling down the counter, grinning in that way John knew so well, since he himself had done it so many times with other guys, when they knew they had some guy in a corner. The Woolworth man winked at them.

Inspired by embarrassment, John came up with an idea. "It's not for a girl," he lied; "it's for my mother."

He managed to look at old squinch-eye steadily, but
his voice gave him away and he knew it. Just the
same, he knew that not even these guys would dare
make fun about anything as sacred as a guy's mother,
so it was a good lie.

The Woolworth man seemed to be a little non-
plused. There was a short pause as everybody stopped
riding him and thought solemnly of their own sacred
mothers. It made John think suddenly of how Cath-
olics looked when they passed a church and stopped
and crossed themselves. Then old squinch-eye, having
paused respectfully, winked at the two guys and said,
"Aw, come on, Johnny. You can tell us. Who is she?
Really."

"Yeah, come on and tell us," one of the guys, Ted
Wright, said.

"Yeah. We'll find out anyway, Slade," the other one,
Hank Lewis, said, grinning.

"I told you," John said as stoutly as he could. "I
ain't got a girl. This is for my mom." The box was
wrapped now, but old squinch-eye was reluctant to
let go of it and spoil the fun. John took the folded
bills, seven dollars in all, that he had been saving out
of his route (he had even made a special trip around,
when he wasn't carrying, to collect some of the back
bills, so he would have enough) from his pocket and
extended them, and at the same time held out his
other hand.

The Woolworth man passed over the package with
his right hand and took the money with his left, but
then he would not quite let go. His hand clung to the
box of candy teasingly.

"Is she in your room?" he asked. "Is she in 8A?
Come on, you call tell *us.*"

"Maybe she's in 8B," one of the guys said. "Maybe
she's from down in Sacktown."

"Yeah. Maybe it's one of the Linder girls," the
other one grinned. "Is it one of the Linder girls,
Johnny?"

"I told you," John said. "Can I have my change,
please?"

Finally, reluctantly, old squinch-eye let go of the box. "Your change? A whole nickel? I'm not sure I've got that much on hand." But he turned around to the register, and then finally the ordeal was over. How could any guy get to be so mean, in just thirty years or so?

Trying hard not to walk too fast, aware of his chest rising and falling fast and his arms and legs trembling, and hoping none of it showed, John went to the door with as much dignity as he could muster up.

"We'll find out anyway, Slade," one of the guys called after him. "We'll find out anyway; tomorrow."

And they would, too. It was a threatening promise of what he could expect.

Outside, he laid the wrapped package carefully in the basket of his bike, kicked up the stand and pushed off, swinging his leg over the rear wheel. Well, to hell with them. Let them find out. Let them find out he was in love with (oh, sweet, lovely name!) Margaret Simpson. He didn't care. He was proud of it. So let them find out. They would anyway.

At home, he went straight upstairs to his own room and put the wrapped box carefully away in a drawer of his dresser, and he did not tell anybody, neither his parents nor his kid sister, about it. But that night, after supper and the radio and homework and some reading, when he went to bed, he lay with his arms behind his head and thought about it. Finally he got up and took it out and unwrapped it (he could put it in a paper bag tomorrow to keep it clean—and hidden) and looked at it. He was both excited and scared about tomorrow. He wished there *was* somebody he could talk to about it. He hoped it would be all right, and he *thought* it would. Certainly it would be the best, the most expensive valentine any girl in the class would get. That was for sure. But you couldn't be sure with Margaret. She was a pretty sophisticated girl. Love and desire for her welled up in him at the silent pronunciation of her name, and he put the box carefully away and climbed back into bed.

Actually, he had never spoken to Margaret about his feeling for her. Maybe he should have. His *love* for her, he corrected himself. (And of course there were some things he *couldn't* speak to her about. Sex thoughts. The very idea made his face feel flushed and made him feel guilty. He shouldn't even feel that about her. But then, the two things were entirely different, weren't they? They didn't really have anything to do with each other at all, did they?) His *love*, he said again. Actually, she was easily the most popular girl in the class, and had been elected most popular girl last year in seventh grade, and undoubtedly would be again this year in eighth grade, as well as being the best-looking. She wore lots of skirts and sweaters, with the sleeves pushed up, and she had the best-developed chest in 8A. Actually, she came from a very poor family, and lived in a very poor tacky little house on the far side of town. Her mother was dead and she kept house for her father and those of her five big brothers who still lived at home, which was two. Actually, she was really much better-off than that sounded, because old Mrs. Carter, who was rich and had a sort of estate right next door to Margaret's home, had taken her under her wing and paid for all her clothes and things and was going to send her to college. Also, all her five brothers were musical, as she was herself, and played instruments and had played in bands around town, and so Margaret herself had been singing with a band that one of her brothers ran, at places like the Elks Club and the Country Club, ever since she had been in sixth grade. That, right there, probably accounted for a lot of her sophistication. Everybody said she was really very talented as a singer and might have a chance to go a long way someday. Also she made excellent grades; always.

Well, he bet she had never had as expensive, or as big, a valentine as this before, even from a sophomore; and thinking about her in the warmth of the bed, under the warm covers, John rolled over and, still worried, curled himself up and went to sleep.

Once, almost two years ago, during the summer after sixth grade, he had tried to make love to another girl. This girl was two years younger than him, the same age as his kid sister, and she lived across the street and they all used to play together a lot, with all the other kids from the block. But one night, after dark, just the three of them—his sister, this girl and himself—were sitting on this girl's porch across the street. The porch light was out, so it was dark, and he and the little girl were in the swing, and his sister was in a chair not far from them. All afternoon and all evening, when they'd been playing, this little girl had been poking him and pinching him and grabbing him and tickling him and accidentally falling against him, and then giggling. He had assumed from this that she liked him and was giving him a sort of invitation, so in the swing in the dark, strangely excited, he put his arm around her and whispered to her to let him kiss her. Actually, he didn't even get his arm completely around her because she moved away from him before he could; and though she had been warm and practically rubbing herself against him, she was now suddenly cold and untouchable. Still excited, in a way he had never felt before, he slid over after her in the swing and tried again, tried several times, whispering for her to please let him kiss her, with the same result. So, knowing vaguely that this was what adults did in similar circumstances and feeling dimly that there must be some magic open-sesame in the words themselves, he whispered. "I love you." It was the first time he had ever said the words, except possibly to his mother. They did not, however, open any doors for him. The girl's reaction was forceful and immediate. "You're lovesick," she said accusingly in a voice full of contempt. "That's what you are. You're lovesick." It was a word he had never thought much about or paid any attention to, although when he heard her say it he knew it was a word he had heard before somewhere, and it was clear to him that it was a word she had learned only recently and was using, with a sense of surprised discovery, for the first time. Lovesick.

He had got up out of the swing and left the porch immediately and gone home, leaving the two girls, his sister and the other one, giggling. But instead of going into the house, where he would have had to face his parents, he had gone around behind to the vacant lot next door, where the kids of the block all played, and sat down by himself on the terraced hillside of it, filled with a strange mixture of emotions he had never felt before, but the sum total of which was bad. Very bad, and very sad, and very unhappy. And whenever he thought of the two girls giggling, he felt sick mad all over. It was a beautiful warm summer night, and the stars shimmered overhead with marvelous clarity, and even the Milky Way looked bright. Lovesick. It was like some strange and terrible new disease he had discovered in himself, and he kept saying it over and over to himself: "I'm lovesick. I'm lovesick. I'm lovesick." And he was afflicted with a sense of terrible doom that brought terror and helplessness into him through some opened gate, together with a vague but sure knowledge of forces at work in people that would inevitably, someday, destroy him.

Finally he got up and went into the house to bed, and after that he did not think about the incident often, but whenever he did it brought a sense of shame, and a flush to his face; and the terror, diluted now, would creep back into him, and when he woke up on the morning of Valentine's Day he did not know whether he had dreamed about it during the night or whether he had thought about it just as he was dropping off to sleep, or whether it had just popped into his head for no reason as he was waking up. But he was still worried.

The alarm clock was still ringing, its luminous hands showing four-thirty in the dark, and he shut it off and switched on the light. It was always exciting. Nowhere in the silent, dark house did anything move or stir, nor were there any lights, any movement in any of the houses he could see through his windows as he dressed. Savoring the excitement he felt every morning, he dressed himself warmly—flannel shirt, two sweaters under his Mackinaw, warm socks inside his boots, knit cap down over his ears, heavy scarf—then picked up his heavy fleece-lined leather mittens and tiptoed down the stairs to the front door.

Outside it was steely cold, and the handle bars and sprocket and chain of his bike creaked when he moved them. The air burned his nose like dry ice, and when he tucked the scarf up over it and put on his goggles, his eyes were already watering. The freezing cold air flushing the last threads of sleepiness and reluctance out of his mind, he took off on his bike, giving himself joyously up to, and embracing happily, the discomfort which always made him feel important and as though he were accomplishing something, riding the bike downtown along deserted streets of darkened houses where nothing moved and people slept except for a few boys like himself, scattered across town, converging on the newsstand, where the city papers would already have been picked up off the train by the owner.

Actually, nothing disastrous happened at the newsstand that morning. He was razzed unmercifully by the two who had seen him buy the box the night before, and of course their ridicule was immediately taken up by all the others as they stood at the benches folding their papers and stuffing their paper-bags under the bare bulbs in the back room, but he kept his mouth shut and did not get mad. It was easy to do because he kept a mental picture of Margaret Simpson happily opening the box in the front of his mind, as a shield. Nobody could touch him when he thought of that. Anyway, folding the papers and stacking them took only ten or fifteen minutes, and then the paper boys were outside and separated, spreading out across the town, and he was by himself again, free to enjoy again the physical discomfort that he suffered not only because of the money it made him but because it

made him feel he was strong and had will power, and
also free to dwell upon, and to worry in nervous excitement over, the valentine and his happy picture of
Margaret, as he made his route. Then it was back
home for breakfast and to change for school.

As he was dressing, and as his excitement mounted
to almost unbearably unpleasant heights as the time
slid away, he almost decided to drop the whole thing.
He could leave the box right here in his drawer and
gradually eat the candy up himself. But once again
his ironbound promise to himself, which it was against
his private rules to break, would not let him, and sustained him; that and his happy picture of Margaret
Simpson's face, warm and loving as she opened up his
box, and the natural sequence which automatically followed: of him telling her how much he adored her,
and always had, and her warm understanding of his
adoration, and then his hands touching her. When he
took the box downstairs, hidden in the paper bag,
and his mother asked him what it was, he told her it
was only a couple of books he was taking back.

On the way to school, as the other kids converged,
it was harder to say that. He knew, of course, that the
moment would come (it seemed to be rushing down
on him swiftly, in fact, like a freight train) when it
would have to be made public, when there would be
no avoiding saying what it was, or who it was for. So,
gradually he was forced back to saying simply, "Aw,
nothing," or "Nothing that would interest *you*."
Everybody, of course, knew by now that it was a
valentine.

There were several valentines on his own desk in
the 8A room when he got there, two of them from
girls in the back of the room who thought they were
stuck on him but whom he didn't like because they
both came from Sacktown and were poor, and not
very smart, and often not even very clean. These
valentines he opened and looked at, in a kind of daze,
hardly even seeing them, and then put them down.

Then, painfully aware that he was being watched, he carefully pulled the big box out of its paper bag and laid it on his desk. Big—it was huge! It looked monstrous to him. He had attached a little card which said: *To Margaret, with love, John Slade*. He stared at that awhile. It had cost him deeply in pride and fear to even dare to write it. That word. But he couldn't stare at the envelope forever. Margaret Simpson had not yet come into the room, and the bell wouldn't ring for three and a half minutes. Abruptly, suddenly, he knew he couldn't stand it, just could not wait any longer; he hadn't made a promise to himself he would *hand* it to her, had he? And besides, if he waited to give it to her himself, the way he was now he wouldn't be able to say a word, not a single solitary damned word. Panic had enveloped him. He wanted only to be out of sight of everyone. The valentines on his own desk had given him an idea. Jerkily, cursing himself for looking so foolish, he picked up the box and walked across the room with it and laid it on Margaret Simpson's desk, and then went out into the cloakroom pretending that he had forgotten something in his overcoat.

There was a little buzz, sort of, that he could hear from the cloakroom, and when he peeked around the door there were several kids standing around her desk looking at it, admiring it maybe. He stayed in the cloakroom. How he could manage to stay three whole minutes in the cloakroom he didn't know, and once, as a subterfuge, he went back in to his desk and got some things out of it, pretending he wanted to put them in his coat to take home.

Then, finally, one minute before the bell would ring, Margaret Simpson came into the cloakroom with two boys who were on the grade-school varsity basketball team, and they hung up their coats and went inside. He pretended to be busy with his own coat and did not look at them. Completely demoralized now, no longer able to control what he did, he sneaked to the door and stuck the top half of his head around it, grinning foolishly. Margaret Simpson was just showing the card, his card, to the two boys. She said something he could not hear, and then laughed and gestured with her head toward the cloakroom where he was hiding, and the two boys laughed. Then she looked down at the big red box with amusement.

He had seen enough and he jerked his head back and crept back to his own coat, pretending to himself he had to get something out of the pocket. But then he leaned his face against his coat sickly and shut his eyes, trying to shut out not only the light but his own existence too. He put his hand in the pocket of the coat so that it would look like he was hunting for something in case anybody came in. When the bell rang, how could he ever go back in there? How could he possibly? Sickness ran all through him, all over him, in long waves. And everybody had seen him peeking around the doorjamb like a silly idiot. He had ruined it. He'd messed it all up. He should have made himself stay and hand it to her. Then it would have been all right. He stood that way, clenching and unclenching his fists, knowing the bell would ring, listening for it.

When the bell rang, he forced himself to walk to the door and to his desk. He sat down, trying hard not to look at anybody. Before the bell rang again, he would have to sit at that desk for fifty whole minutes of his life.

A Sense of Shelter

BY JOHN UPDIKE

SNOW FELL against the high school all day, wet big-flaked snow that did not accumulate well. Sharpening two pencils, William looked down on a parking lot that was a blackboard in reverse, car tires had cut smooth arcs of black into the white, and wherever a school bus had backed around, it had left an autocratic signature of two V's. The snow, though at moments it whirled opaquely, could not quite bleach these scars away. The temperature must be exactly 32°. The window was open a crack, and a canted pane of glass lifted outdoor air into his face, coating the cedar-wood scent of pencil shavings with the transparent odor of the wet window sill. With each revolution of the handle his knuckles came within a fraction of an inch of the tilted glass, and the faint chill this prox-imity breathed on them sharpened his already acute sense of shelter.

The sky behind the shreds of snow was stone-colored. The murk inside the high classroom gave the air a solidity that limited the overhead radiance to its own vessels; six globes of dull incandescence floated on the top of a thin sea. The feeling the gloom gave him was not gloomy but joyous: he felt they were all sealed in, safe; the colors of cloth were dyed deeper, the sound of whispers was made more distinct, the smells of tablet paper and wet shoes and varnish and face powder pierced him with a vivid sense of pos-session. These were his classmates sealed in, his, the stupid as well as the clever, the plain as well as the lovely, his enemies as well as his friends, his. He felt

67

like a king and seemed to move to his seat between
the bowed heads of subjects that loved him less than
he loved them. His seat was sanctioned by tradition;
for twelve years he had sat at the rear of classrooms,
William Young, flanked by Marsha Wyckoff and Andy
Zimmerman. Once there had been two Zimmermans,
but one went to work in his father's greenhouse, and
in some classes—Latin and Trig—there were none, and
William sat at the edge of the class as if on the lip of a
cliff, and Marsha Wyckoff became Marvin Wolf or
Sandra Wade, but it was always the same desk, whose
surface altered from hour to hour but from whose
blue-stained ink-hole his mind could extract, like a
chain of magicians' handkerchiefs, a continuity of
years. As a senior he was a kind of king, and as a
teacher's pet another kind, a puppet king, who gathered in appointive posts and even, when the moron
vote split between two football heroes, some elective
ones. He was not popular, he had never had a girl, his
intense friends of childhood had drifted off into teams
and gangs, and in large groups—when the whole
school, for instance, went in the fall to the beautiful,
dung-and-cotton-candy-smelling county fair—he was
always an odd man, without a seat on the bus home.
But exclusion is itself a form of inclusion. He even
had a nickname: Mip, because he stuttered. Taunts no
longer much frightened him; he had come late into
his physical inheritance, but this summer it had arrived, and he at last stood equal with his enormous,
boisterous parents, and had to unbutton his shirt cuffs
to get his wrists through them, and discovered he
could pick up a basketball with one hand. So, his long
legs blocking two aisles, he felt regal even in size and,
almost trembling with happiness under the high globes
of light beyond whose lunar glow invisible snowflakes
were drowning on the gravel roof of his castle, believed that the long delay of unpopularity had been
merely a consolidation, that he was at last strong
enough to make his move. Today he would tell Mary
Landis he loved her.

He had loved her ever since, a fat-faced tomboy

with freckles and green eyes, she deftly stole his rubber-lined schoolbag on the walk back from second grade along Jewett Street and outran him—simply had better legs. The superior speed a boy was supposed to have failed to come; his kidneys burned with panic. In front of the grocery store next to her home she stopped and turned. She was willing to have him catch up. This humiliation on top of the rest was too much to bear. Tears broke in his throat; he spun around and ran home and threw himself on the floor of the front parlor, where his grandfather, feet twiddling, perused the newspaper and soliloquized all morning. In time the letter slot rustled, and the doorbell rang, and Mary gave his mother the schoolbag and the two of them politely exchanged whispers. Their voices had been to him, lying there on the carpet with his head wrapped in his arms, indistinguishable. Mother had always liked Mary. From when she had been a tiny girl dancing along the hedge on the end of an older sister's arm, Mother had liked her. Out of all the children that flocked, similar as pigeons, through the neighborhood, Mother's heart had reached out with claws and fastened on Mary. He never took the schoolbag to school again, had refused to touch it. He supposed it was still in the attic, still faintly smelling of sweet pink rubber.

Fixed high on the plaster like a wren clinging to a barn wall, the buzzer sounded the two-minute signal. In the middle of the classroom Mary Landis stood up, a Monitor badge pinned to her belly. Her broad red belt was buckled with a brass bow and arrow. She wore a lavender sweater with the sleeves pushed up to expose her forearms, a delicately cheap effect. Wild stories were told about her; perhaps it was merely his knowledge of these that put the hardness in her face. Her eyes seemed braced for squinting and their green was frosted. Her freckles had faded. William thought she laughed less this year; now that she was in the Secretarial Course and he in the College Preparatory, he saw her in only one class a day, this one, English. She stood a second, eclipsed at the thighs by Jack

Stephens' zebra-striped shoulders, and looked back at
the class with a stiff worn glance, as if she had seen
the same faces too many times before. Her habit of
perfect posture emphasized the angularity she had
grown into. There was a nervous edge, a boxiness in
her bones, that must have been waiting all along under
the childish fat. Her eye sockets were deeply indented
and her chin had a prim square set that seemed in the
murky air tremulous and defiant. Her skirt was cut
square and straight. Below the waist she was lean;
the legs that had outrun him were still athletic; she
starred at hockey and cheerleading. Above, she was
abundant: so stacked her spine curved backwards
to keep her body balanced. She turned and in switch-
ing up the aisle encountered a boy's leg thrown into
her path. She coolly looked down until it withdrew.
She was used to such attentions. Her pronged chest
poised, Mary proceeded out the door, and someone
she saw in the hall made her smile, a wide smile full of
warmth and short white teeth, and love scooped at
William's heart. He would tell her.

In another minute, the second bell rasped. Shuf-
fling through the perfumed crowds to his next class,
he crooned to himself in the slow, over-enunciated
manner of the Negro vocalist who had brought the
song back this year:

> "Lah-vender blue, dilly dilly,
> Lavendih gree-heen;
> *Eef* I were king, dilly dilly,
> You would: be queen."

The song gave him an exultant sliding sensation
that intertwined with the pleasures of his day. He
knew all the answers, he had done all the work, the
teachers called upon him only to rebuke the ignorance of the others. In Trig and Soc Sci both it was
this way. In gym, the fourth hour of the morning, he,
who was always picked near the last, startled his side
by excelling at volleyball, leaping like a madman,
shouting like a bully. The ball felt light as a feather

against his big bones. His hair in wet quills from the shower, he walked in the icy air to Luke's Luncheonette, where he ate three hamburgers in a booth with three juniors. There was Barry Kruppman, a tall, thyroid-eyed boy who came on the school bus from the country town of Bowsville and who was an amateur hypnotist; he told the tale of a Portland, Oregon, businessman who under hypnosis had been taken back through sixteen reincarnations to the condition of an Egyptian concubine in the household of a high priest of Isis. There was his friend Lionel Griffin, a pudgy simp whose blond hair pushed out above his ears in two slick waxed wings. He was rumored to be a fairy, and in fact did seem most excited by the transvestite aspect of the soul's transmigration. And there was Lionel's girl Virginia, a drab little mystery who chain-smoked Herbert Tareytons and never said anything. She had sallow skin and smudged eyes and Lionel kept jabbing her and shrieking, making William wince. He would rather have sat with members of his own class, who filled the other booths, but he would have had to force himself on them. These juniors admired him and welcomed his company. He asked, "Wuh-well, was he ever a c-c-c-cockroach, like Archy?"

Kruppman's face grew intense; his furry lids dropped down over the bulge of his eyes, and when they drew back, his pupils were as small and hard as BBs. "That's the really interesting thing. There was this gap, see, between his being a knight under Charlemagne and then a sailor on a ship putting out from Macedonia—that's where Yugoslavia is now—in the time of Nero; there was this gap, when the only thing the guy would do was walk around the office snarling and growling, see, like this." Kruppman worked his blotched ferret face up into a snarl and Griffin shrieked. "He tried to bite one of the assistants and they think that for six hundred years"—the uncanny, unhealthy seriousness of his whisper hushed Griffin momentarily—"for six hundred years he just was a series of wolves. Probably in the German forests.

You see, when he was in Macedonia"—his whisper
barely audible—"he murdered a woman."

Griffin squealed in ecstasy and cried, "Oh, Kruppman! Kruppman, how you do go on!" and jabbed
Virginia in the arm so hard a Herbert Tareyton
jumped from her hand and bobbled across the Formica
table. William gazed over their heads in pain.

The crowds at the soda counter had thinned so that
when the door to the outside opened he saw Mary
come in and hesitate there for a second where the
smoke inside and the snow outside swirled together.
The mixture made a kind of—Kruppman's ridiculous
story had put the phrase in his head—wolf-weather,
and she was just a gray shadow caught in it alone.
She bought a pack of cigarettes from Luke and went
out again, a kerchief around her head, the pneumatic
thing above the door hissing behind her. For a long
time, always in fact, she had been at the center of
whatever gang was the one: in the second grade the
one that walked home up Jewett Street together, and
in the sixth grade the one that went bicycling as far
away as the quarry and the Rentschler estate and
played touch football Saturday afternoons, and in the
ninth grade the one that went roller-skating at Can-
dlebridge Park with the tenth-grade boys, and in the
eleventh grade the one that held parties lasting past
midnight and that on Sundays drove in caravans as
far as Philadelphia and back. And all the while there
had been a succession of boy friends, first Jack
Stephens and Fritz March in their class and then boys
a grade ahead and then Barrel Lord, who was a senior
when they were sophomores and whose name was in
the newspapers all football season, and then this last
summer someone out of the school altogether, a man
she met while working as a waitress in the city of
Alton. So this year her weekends were taken up, and
the party gang carried on as if she had never existed,
and nobody saw her much except in school and when
she stopped by in Luke's to buy a pack of cigarettes.
Her silhouette against the big window had looked
wan, her head hooded, her face nibbled by light, her

fingers fiddling on the veined counter with her coins. He yearned to reach out, to comfort her, but he was wedged deep in the shrill booths, between the jingling guts of the pinball machine and the hillbilly joy of the jukebox. The impulse left him with a disagreeable feeling. He had loved her too long to want to pity her; it endangered the investment of worship on which he had not yet realized any return.

The two hours of the school afternoon held Latin and a study hall. In study hall, while the five people at the table with him played tic-tac-toe and sucked cough drops and yawned, he did all his homework for the next day. He prepared thirty lines of Vergil, Aeneas in the Underworld. The study hall was a huge low room in the basement of the building; its coziness crept into Tartarus. On the other side of the fudge-colored wall the circular saw in the woodworking shop whined and gasped and then whined again; it bit off pieces of wood with a rising, somehow terrorized inflection—bzzzzzup! He solved ten problems in trigonometry. His mind cut neatly through their knots and separated them, neat stiff squares of answer, one by one from the long but finite plank of problems that connected Plane Geometry with Solid. Lastly, as the snow on a ragged slant drifted down into the cement pits outside the steel-mullioned windows, he read a short story by Edgar Allan Poe. He closed the book softly on the pleasing sonority of its final note of horror, gazed at the red, wet, menthol-scented inner membrane of Judy Whipple's yawn, rimmed with flaking pink lipstick, and yielded his conscience to the snug sense of his work done, of the snow falling, of the warm minutes that walked through their shelter so slowly. The perforated acoustic tiling above his head seemed the lining of a long tube that would go all the way: high school merging into college, college into graduate school, graduate school into teaching at a college—section man, assistant, associate, *full* professor, possessor of a dozen languages and a thousand books, a man brilliant in his forties, wise in his fifties, renowned in his sixties, revered in his seventies, and then retired, sitting in the study lined with acoustical books until the time came for the last transition from silence to silence, and he would die, like Tennyson, with a copy of *Cymbeline* beside him on the moon-drenched bed.

After school he had to go to Room 101 and cut a sports cartoon into a stencil for the school paper. He liked the building best when it was nearly empty, when the casual residents—the rural commuters, the do-nothings, the trash—had cleared out. Then the janitors went down the halls sowing seeds of red wax and making an immaculate harvest with broad brooms, gathering all the fluff and hairpins and wrappers and powder that the animals had dropped that day. The basketball team thumped in the hollow gymnasium; the cheerleaders rehearsed behind drawn curtains on the stage. In Room 101 two empty-headed typists with stripes bleached into their hair banged away between giggles and mistakes. At her desk Mrs. Gregory, the faculty sponsor, wearily passed her pencil through misspelled news copy on tablet paper. William took the shadow box from the top of the filing cabinet and the styluses and little square plastic shading screens from their drawer and the stencil from the closet where the typed stencils hung, like fragile scarves, on hooks. B-BALLERS BOW, 57-42, was the headline. He drew a tall b-baller bowing to a stumpy pagan idol, labelled "W" for victorious Weiserton High, and traced it in the soft blue wax with the fine loop stylus. His careful breath grazed his knuckles. His eyebrows frowned while his heart bobbed happily on the giddy prattle of the typists. The shadow box was simply a black frame holding a pane of glass and lifted at one end by two legs so the light bulb, fitted in a tin tray, could slide under; it was like a primitive lean-to sheltering a fire. As he worked, his eyes smarting, he mixed himself up with the light bulb, felt himself burning under a slanting roof upon which a huge hand scratched. The glass grew hot; the danger in the job was pulling the softened wax with your damp hand, distorting or tearing the typed letters. Sometimes the center of an *o* stuck to your skin like a bit of blue confetti. But he was expert and cautious. He returned the things to their places feeling airily tall, heightened by Mrs. Gregory's appreciation, which she expressed by keeping her back turned, in effect stating that other staff members were undependable but William did not need to be watched.

In the hall outside Room 101 only the shouts of a basketball scrimmage reverberated; the chant of the cheerleaders had been silenced. Though he had done everything, he felt reluctant to leave. Neither of his parents—both worked—would be home yet, and this building was as much his home. He knew all its nooks. On the second floor of the annex, beyond the art room, there was a strange, narrow boys' lavatory that no one ever seemed to use. It was here one time that Barry Kruppman tried to hypnotize him and cure his stuttering. Kruppman's voice purred and his irises turned tiny in the bulging whites and for a moment William felt himself lean backward involuntarily, but he was distracted by the bits of bloodshot pink in the corners of these portentous eyes; the folly of giving up his will to an intellectual inferior occurred to him; he refused to let go and go under, and perhaps therefore his stuttering had continued.

The frosted window at the end of the long room cast a watery light on the green floor and made the porcelain urinals shine like slices of moon. The semiopacity of this window gave the room's air of secrecy great density. William washed his hands with exaggerated care, enjoying the lavish amount of powdered soap provided for him in this castle. He studied his face in the mirror, making infinitesimal adjustments to attain the absolutely most flattering angle, and then put his hands below his throat to get their strong, long-fingered beauty into the picture. As he walked toward the door he sang, closing his eyes and gasping as if he were a real Negro whose entire career depended upon this recording:

"Who—told me so, dilly dilly,

Who told me soho?
Aii told myself, dilly dilly,
I told: me so."

When he emerged into the hall it was not empty:
one girl walked down its varnished perspective toward
him, Mary Landis, a scarf on her head and books in
her arms. Her locker was up here, on the second floor
of the annex. His own was in the annex basement. A
tickling sensation that existed neither in the medium
of sound nor of light crowded against his throat. She
flipped the scarf back from her hair and in a con-
versational voice that carried well down the clean
planes of the hall said, "Hi, Billy." The name came
from way back, when they were both children, and
made him feel small but brave.

"Hi. How are you?"

"Fine." Her smile broadened out from the *F* of this
word.

What was so funny? Was she really, as it seemed,
pleased to see him? "Du-did you just get through
cheer-cheer-cheer-leading?"

"Yes. Thank God. *Oh* she's so awful. She makes us
do the same stupid locomotives for every cheer; I told
her, no wonder nobody cheers any more."

"This is M-M-Miss Potter?" He blushed, feeling that
he made an ugly face in getting past the *M*. When he
got caught in the middle of a sentence the constric-
tion was somehow worse. He admired the way words
poured up her throat, distinct and petulant.

"Yes, Potbottom Potter," she said, "she's just aching
for a man and takes it out on us. I wish she would
get one. Honestly, Billy, I have half a mind to quit. I'll
be so glad when June comes, I'll never set foot in this
idiotic building again."

Her lips, pale with the lipstick worn off, crinkled
bitterly. Her face, foreshortened from the height of
his eyes, looked cross as a cat's. It a little shocked him
that poor Miss Potter and this kind, warm school
stirred her to what he had to take as actual anger; this
grittiness in her was the first abrasive texture he had

struck today. Couldn't she see around teachers, into their fatigue, their poverty, their fear? It had been so long since he had spoken to her, he wasn't sure how coarse she had become. "Don't quit," he brought out of his mouth at last. "It'd be n-n-n-nuh—it'd be nothing without you."

He pushed open the door at the end of the hall for her and as she passed under his arm she looked up and said, "Why, aren't you sweet?"

The stairwell, all asphalt and iron, smelled of galoshes. It felt more secret than the hall, more specially theirs; there was something magical in its shifting multiplicity of planes as they descended that lifted the spell on his tongue, so that words came as quickly as his feet pattered on the steps.

"No I mean it," he said, "you're really a beautiful cheerleader. But then you're beautiful period."

"I've skinny legs."

"Who told you that?"

"Somebody."

"Well *he* wasn't very sweet."

"No."

"Why do you hate this poor old school?"

"Now Billy. You know you don't care about this junky place any more than I do."

"I love it. It breaks my heart to hear you say you want to get out, because then I'll never see you again."

"You don't care, do you?"

"Why sure I care; you *know*"—their feet stopped; they had reached bottom, the first-floor landing, two brass-barred doors and a grimy radiator—"I've always li-loved you."

"You don't mean that."

"I do too. It's ridiculous but there it is. I wanted to tell you today and now I have."

He expected her to laugh and go out the door, but instead she showed an unforseeable willingness to discuss this awkward matter. He should have realized before this that women enjoy being talked to. "It's a very silly thing to say," she asserted tentatively.

"I don't see why," he said, fairly bold now that he

couldn't seem more ridiculous, and yet picking his
words with a certain strategic care. "It's not *that* silly
to love somebody, I mean what the hell. Probably
what's silly is not to do anything about it for umpteen
years but then I never had an opportunity, I thought."

He set his books down on the radiator and she set
hers down beside his. "What kind of opportunity were
you waiting for?"

"Well, see, that's it; I didn't know." He wished, in
a way, she would go out the door. But she had propped
herself against the wall and plainly awaited more talking. "Yuh-you were such a queen and I was such a
nothing and I just didn't really want to presume." It
wasn't very interesting; it puzzled him that she seemed
to be interested. Her face had grown quite stern, the
mouth very small and thoughtful, and he made a gesture with his hands intended to release her from the
bother of thinking about it; after all, it was just a
disposition of his heart, nothing permanent or expensive; perhaps it was just his mother's idea anyway.
Half in impatience to close the account, he asked,
"Will you marry me?"

"You don't want to marry me," she said. "You're
going to go on and be a great man."

He blushed in pleasure; is this how she saw him, is
this how they all saw him; as worthless now, but in
time a great man? Had his hopes always been on
view? He dissembled, saying, "No I'm not. But anyway, you're great now. You're so pretty, Mary."

"Oh, Billy," she said, "if you were me for just one
day you'd hate it."

She said this rather blankly, watching his eyes; he
wished her voice had shown more misery. In his world
of closed surfaces a panel, carelessly pushed, had
opened, and he hung in this openness paralyzed, unable to think what to say. Nothing he could think of
quite fit the abruptly immense context. The radiator
cleared its throat; its heat made, in the intimate volume
just this side of the doors on whose windows the snow
beat limply, a provocative snugness; he supposed he
should try, and stepped forward, his hands lifting to-

ward her shoulders. Mary sidestepped between him and the radiator and put the scarf back on. She lifted the cloth like a broad plaid halo above her head and then wrapped it around her chin and knotted it so she looked, in her red galoshes and bulky coat, like a peasant woman in a movie of Europe. With her thick hair swathed, her face seemed pale and chunky, and when she recradled the books in her arms her back bent humbly under the point of the kerchief. "It's too hot in here," she said. "I've got to wait for somebody." The disconnectedness of the two statements seemed natural in the fragmented atmosphere his stops and starts had produced. She bucked the brass bar with her shoulder and the door slammed open; he followed her into the weather.

"For the person who thinks your legs are too skinny?"

"Uh-huh." As she looked up at him a snowflake caught on the lashes of one eye. She jerkily rubbed that cheek on the shoulder of her coat and stamped a foot, splashing slush. Cold water gathered on the back of his thin shirt. He put his hands in his pockets and pressed his arms against his sides to keep from shivering.

"Thuh-then you wo-won't marry me?" His wise instinct told him the only way back was by going forward, through absurdity.

"We don't know each other," she said.

"My God," he said. "Why not? I've known you since I was two."

"What do you know about me?"

This awful seriousness of hers; he must dissolve it. "That you're not a virgin." But instead of making her laugh this made her face go dead and turned it away. Like beginning to kiss her, it was a mistake; in part, he felt grateful for his mistakes. They were like loyal friends who are nevertheless embarrassing. "What do you know about *me?*" he asked, setting himself up for a finishing insult but dreading it. He hated the stiff feel of his smile between his cheeks; glimpsed, as if the snow were a mirror, how hateful he looked.

"That you're basically very nice."

Her returning good for evil blinded him to his physical discomfort, set him burning with regret. "Listen," he said, "I did love you. Let's at least get that straight."

"You never loved anybody," she said. "You don't know what it is."

"O.K." he said. "Pardon me."

"You're excused."

"You better wait in the school," he told her. "He's-eez-eez going to be a long time."

She didn't answer and walked a little distance, toe-ing out in the childish Dutch way common to the women in this county, along the slack cable that divided the parking lot from the softball field. One bicycle, rusted as if it had been there for years, leaned in the rack, its fenders supporting airy crescents of white.

The warmth inside the door felt heavy. William picked up his books and ran his pencil along the black ribs of the radiator before going down the stairs to his locker in the annex basement. The shadows were thick at the foot of the steps; suddenly it felt late, he must hurry and get home. He was seized by the irrational fear that they were going to lock him in. The cloistered odors of paper, sweat, and, from the woodshop at the far end of the basement hall, saw-dust no longer flattered him. The tall green double lockers appeared to study him critically through the three air slits near their tops. When he opened his locker, and put his books on his shelf, below Marvin Wolf's, and removed his coat from his hook, his self seemed to crawl into the long dark space thus made vacant, the humiliated ugly, educable self. In answer to a flick of his great hand the steel door weightlessly floated shut and through the length of his body he felt so clean and free he smiled. Between now and the happy future predicted for him he had nothing, almost literally nothing, to do.

Michael Egerton

BY REYNOLDS PRICE

HE WAS the first boy I met at camp. He had got there before me, and he and a man were taking things out of a suitcase when I walked into the cabin. He came over and started talking right away without even knowing me. He even shook hands. I don't think I had ever shaken hands with anyone my own age before. Not that I minded. I was just surprised and had to find a place to put my duffel bag before I could give him my hand. His name was Michael, Michael Egerton. He was taller than I was, and although it was only June, he already had the sort of suntan that would leave his hair white all summer. I knew he couldn't be more than twelve. I wouldn't be twelve until February. If you were twelve you usually had to go to one of the senior cabins across the hill. But his face was old because of the bones under his eyes that showed through the skin.

He introduced me to the man. It was his father but they didn't look alike. His father was a newspaperman and the suitcase they were unpacking had stickers on it that said Rome and Paris, London and Bombay. His father said he would be going back to Europe soon to report about the Army and that Michael would be settled here in camp for a while. I was to keep an eye on Mike, he said, and if he got to France in time, he would try to send us something. He said he could tell that Mike and I were going to be great friends and that I might want to go with Mike to his aunt's when camp was over. I might like to see where Old Mike would be living from now on. It was a beautiful place,

he said. I could tell he was getting ready to leave. He
had seen Michael make up his bed and fill the locker
with clothes, and he was beginning to talk the way
everybody does when they are leaving somewhere—
loud and with a lot of laughing.

He took Michael over to a corner, and I started unpacking my bag. I could see them though and he
gave Michael some money, and they talked about
how much Michael was going to enjoy the summer
and how much bigger he would be when his father
got back and how he was to think of his aunt just
like a mother. Then Michael reached up and kissed his
father. He didn't seem at all embarrassed to do it. They
walked back towards me and in a voice louder than
before, Mr. Egerton told me again to keep an eye on
Old Mike—not that he would need it but it wouldn't
hurt. That was a little funny since Michael was so
much bigger than I was, but anyway I said I would
because that was what I was supposed to say. And
then he left. He said there wouldn't be any need for
Mike to walk with him to the car, but Michael wanted
to so I watched them walk down the hill together.
They stood by the car for a minute, and then Michael
kissed him again right in front of all those boys and
parents and counselors. Michael stood there until his
father's car had passed through the camp gate. He
waved once. Then he came on back up the hill.

All eight of the boys in our cabin went to the dining hall together that night, but afterward at campfire Michael and I sat a little way off from the others
and talked softly while they sang. He talked some
about his father and how he was one of the best war
correspondents in the business. It wasn't like bragging
because he asked me about my father and what my
mother was like. I started to ask him about his mother,
but I remembered that he hadn't said anything about
her, and I thought she might be dead. But in a while
he said very matter-of-factly that his mother didn't
live with him and his father, hadn't lived with them

for almost a year. That was all. He hadn't seen his mother for a year. He didn't say whether she was sick or what, and I wasn't going to ask.

For a long time after that we didn't say anything. We were sitting on a mound at the foot of a tree just high enough to look down on the other boys around the fire. They were all red in the light, and those furthest from the blaze huddled together and drew their heads down because the nights in the mountains were cold, even in June. They had started singing a song that I didn't know. It was called "Green Grow the Rushes." But Michael knew it and sang and I listened to him. It was almost like church with one person singing against a large soft choir. At the end the camp director stood up and made a speech about this was going to be the best season in the history of Redwood which was the finest camp in the land as it was bound to be with as fine a group of boys and counselors as he had sitting right here in front of him. He said it would be a perfect summer if everybody would practice the Golden Rule twenty-four hours a day and treat everybody like we wanted to be treated— like real men.

When we got back to the cabin, the other boys were already running around in the lantern light naked and slapping each other's behinds with wet towels. But soon the counselor blew the light out, and we got in bed in the dark. Michael was in the bunk over me. We had sentence prayers. Michael asked God to bless his father when he got to France. One boy named Robin Mickle who was a Catholic said a Hail Mary. It surprised most of the others. Some of them even laughed as if he was telling a joke. Everything quieted down though and we were half asleep when somebody started blowing Taps on a bugle. It woke us all up and we waited in the dark for it to stop so we could sleep.

Michael turned out to be my best friend. Every morning after breakfast everybody was supposed to lie on their beds quietly for Thought Time and think about the Bible, but Michael and I would sit on my bed and talk. I told Michael a lot of things I had never told anyone else. I don't know why I told him. I just wanted him to know everything there was to know about me. It was a long time before I realized that I didn't know much about Michael except what I could see—that he didn't live with his mother and his father was a great war correspondent who was probably back in France now. He just wasn't the kind to tell you a lot. He would listen to everything you had to say as if he wanted to hear it and was glad you wanted to tell him. But then he would change the subject and start talking about baseball or something. He was a very good baseball player, the best on the junior cabin team. Every boy in our cabin was on the team, and it looked as if with Michael pitching we might take the junior title for the Colossians. That was the name of our team. All the athletic teams in camp were named for one of the letters that St. Paul wrote. We practiced every afternoon after rest period, but first we went to the Main Lodge for mail. I got a letter almost every day, and Michael had got two or three from his aunt, but it wasn't until almost three weeks passed that he got the airmail letter from France. There weren't any pictures or souvenirs in it, but I don't suppose Mr. Egerton had too much time for that. He did mention me though I could tell by the way he wrote that he didn't remember my name. Still it was very nice to be thought of by a famous war correspondent. Michael said we could write him a letter together soon and that he would ask his father for a picture.

We wrote him twice but four weeks passed and nothing else came, not from France. I had any number of letters myself and the legal limit of boxes (which was one a week) that I wanted to share with just Michael but had to share with everybody, Robin Mickle included. Worse than the sharing, I dreaded

my boxes because I kept thinking they would make
me homesick, but with Michael and all the things to
do, they never bothered me, and before I expected it,
there was only a week of camp left and we would
go home. That was why we were playing the semi-
finals that day—so the winners could be recognized
at the Farewell Banquet on the last night of camp.
The Colossians were going to play the Ephesians after
rest period. We were all in the cabin trying to rest,
but everybody was too excited, everybody except Michael who was almost asleep when the camp director
walked in and said that Michael Egerton was to go
down to the Lodge porch right away as he had visi-
tors. Michael got up and combed his hair, and just
before he left he told everybody he would see them
at the game and that we were going to win.

The Lodge wasn't too far from our cabin, and I
could see him walking down there. A car was parked
by the porch. Michael got pretty close to it. Then he
stopped. I thought he had forgotten something and
was coming back to the cabin, but the car doors
opened and a man and a woman got out. I knew it
was his mother. He couldn't have looked any more
like her. She bent over and kissed him. Then she must
have introduced him to the man. She said something
and the man stepped up and shook Michael's hand.
They started talking. I couldn't hear them and since
they weren't doing anything I lay back down and
read for a while. Rest period was almost over when
I looked again. The car was gone and there was no
one in front of the Lodge. It was time for the semi-
finals, and Michael hadn't showed up. Robin, who
was in charge of the Colossians, told me to get Michael wherever he was, and I looked all over camp. He
just wasn't there. I didn't have time to go up in the
woods behind the cabins, but I yelled and there was
no answer. So I had to give up because the game was
waiting. Michael never came. A little fat boy named
Billy Joe Moffitt took his place and we lost. Everybody wondered what had happened to Michael. I was
sure he hadn't left camp with his mother because he

would have told somebody first so after the game I ran back ahead of the others. Michael wasn't on his bed. I walked through the hall and opened the bathroom door. He was standing at the window with his back to me. "Mike, why in the world didn't you play?"

He didn't even turn around.

"We lost, Mike."

He just stood there tying little knots in the shade cord. When the others came in from the game, I met them at the door. I told them Michael was sick.

But he went to the campfire with me that night. He didn't say much and I didn't know what to ask him. "Was that your mother this afternoon?"

"Yes."

"What was she doing up here?"

"On a vacation or something."

I don't guess I should have asked him but I did. "Who was that with her?"

"Some man. I don't know. Just some man."

It was like every night. We were sitting in our place by the tree. The others were singing and we were listening. Then he started talking very fast.

"My mother said, 'Michael, this is your new father. How do you like having two fathers?'"

Before I could think what to say, he said he was cold and got up and walked back to the cabin. I didn't follow him. I didn't even ask him if he was feeling all right. When I got to the cabin, he was in bed pretending to be asleep, but long after Taps I could hear him turning. I tried to stay awake until he went to sleep. Once I sat up and started to reach out and touch him but I didn't. I was very tired.

All that was a week before the end of camp. The boys in our cabin started talking about him. He had stopped playing ball. He wouldn't swim in the camp meet. He didn't even go on the Sunday hike up to

Johnson's Knob. He sat on his bed with his clothes on most of the time. They never did anything nice for him. They were always doing things like tying his shoelaces together. It was no use trying to stop them. All they knew was that Michael Egerton had screwed their chance to be camp baseball champions. They didn't want to know the reason, not even the counselor. And I wasn't going to tell them. They even poured water on his mattress one night and laughed the whole next day about Michael wetting the bed.

The day before we left camp, the counselors voted on a Camp Spirit Cabin. They had kept some sort of record of our activities and athletic events. The cabin with the most Good Camper points usually won. We didn't win. Robin and the others told Michael that he made us lose because he never did anything. They told everybody that Michael Egerton made our cabin lose.

That night we were bathing and getting dressed for the Farewell Banquet. Nobody had expected Michael to go, but without saying anything he started getting dressed. Someone noticed him and said something about Mr. Michael honoring us with his presence at dinner. He had finished dressing when four of the boys took him and tied him between two bunks with his arms stretched out. He didn't fight. He let them treat him like some animal, and he looked as if he was crucified. Then they went to the banquet and left him tied there. I went with them but while they were laughing about hamstringing that damned Michael, I slipped away and went back to untie him. When I got there he had already got loose. I knew he was in the bathroom. I could hear him. I walked to the door and whispered "Mike, it's me." I don't think he heard me. I started to open the door but I didn't. I walked back out and down the hill to the dining hall. They even had the porch lights on, and they had already started singing.

Sucker

BY CARSON MCCULLERS

IT WAS always like I had a room to myself. Sucker slept in my bed with me but that didn't interfere with anything. The room was mine and I used it as I wanted to. Once I remember sawing a trap door in the floor. Last year when I was a sophomore in high school I tacked on my wall some pictures of girls from magazines and one of them was just in her underwear. My mother never bothered me because she had the younger kids to look after. And Sucker thought anything I did was always swell.

Whenever I would bring any of my friends back to my room all I had to do was just glance once at Sucker and he would get up from whatever he was busy with and maybe half smile at me, and leave without saying a word. He never brought kids back there. He's twelve, four years younger than I am, and he always knew without me even telling him that I didn't want kids that age meddling with my things.

Half the time I used to forget that Sucker isn't my brother. He's my first cousin but practically ever since I remember he's been in our family. You see his folks were killed in a wreck when he was a baby. To me and my kid sisters he was like our brother.

Sucker used to always remember and believe every word I said. That's how he got his nick-name. Once a couple of years ago I told him that if he'd jump off our garage with an umbrella it would act as a parachute and he wouldn't fall hard. He did it and busted his knee. That's just one instance. And the funny thing was that no matter how many times he got fooled he would still believe me. Not that he was dumb in other ways—it was just the way he acted with me. He would look at everything I did and quietly take it in.

There is one thing I have learned, but it makes me feel guilty and is hard to figure out. If a person admires you a lot you despise him and don't care—and it is the person who doesn't notice you that you are apt to admire. This is not easy to realize. Maybelle Watts, this senior at school, acted like she was the Queen of Sheba and even humiliated me. Yet at this same time I would have done anything in the world to get her attentions. All I could think about day and night was Maybelle until I was nearly crazy. When Sucker was a little kid and on up until the time he was twelve I guess I treated him as bad as Maybelle did me.

Now that Sucker has changed so much it is a little hard to remember him as he used to be. I never imagined anything would suddenly happen that would make us both very different. I never knew that in order to get what has happened straight in my mind I would want to think back on him as he used to be and compare and try to get things settled. If I could have seen ahead maybe I would have acted different.

I never noticed him much or thought about him and when you consider how long we have had the same room together it is funny the few things I remember. He used to talk to himself a lot when he'd think he was alone—all about him fighting gangsters and being on ranches and that sort of kids' stuff. He'd get in the bathroom and stay as long as an hour and sometimes his voice would go up high and excited and you could hear him all over the house. Usually, though, he was very quiet. He didn't have many boys in the neighborhood to buddy with and his face had the look of a kid who is watching a game and waiting to be asked to play. He didn't mind wearing the sweaters and coats that I outgrew, even if the sleeves did flop down too big and make his wrists look as thin and white as a little girl's. That is how I remem-

ber him—getting a little bigger every year but still
being the same. That was Sucker up until a few
months ago when all this trouble began.

Maybelle was somehow mixed up in what happened
so I guess I ought to start with her. Until I knew her I
hadn't given much time to girls. Last fall she sat next
to me in General Science class and that was when I
first began to notice her. Her hair is the brightest yellow I ever saw and occasionally she will wear it set
into curls with some sort of gluey stuff. Her finger-
nails are pointed and manicured and painted a shiny
red. All during class I used to watch Maybelle, nearly
all the time except when I thought she was going to
look my way or when the teacher called on me. I
couldn't keep my eyes off her hands, for one thing.
They are very little and white except for that red
stuff, and when she would turn the pages of her book
she always licked her thumb and held out her little
finger and turned very slowly. It is impossible to describe Maybelle. All the boys are crazy about her but
she didn't even notice me. For one thing she's almost
two years older than I am. Between periods I used to
try and pass very close to her in the halls but she
would hardly ever smile at me. All I could do was sit
and look at her in class—and sometimes it was like the
whole room could hear my heart beating and I wanted
to holler or light out and run for Hell.

At night, in bed, I would imagine about Maybelle.
Often this would keep me from sleeping until as late
as one or two o'clock. Sometimes Sucker would wake
up and ask me why I couldn't get settled and I'd
tell him to hush his mouth. I suppose I was mean to
him lots of times. I guess I wanted to ignore somebody like Maybelle did me. You could always tell by
Sucker's face when his feelings were hurt. I don't remember all the ugly remarks I must have made because even when I was saying them my mind was on
Maybelle.

That went on for nearly three months and then
somehow she began to change. In the halls she would
speak to me and every morning she copied my home-

work. At lunch time once I danced with her in the
gym. One afternoon I got up nerve and went around
to her house with a carton of cigarettes. I knew she
smoked in the girls' basement and sometimes outside
of school—and I didn't want to take her candy because I think that's been run into the ground. She
was very nice and it seemed to me everything was
going to change.

It was that night when this trouble really started. I
had come into my room late and Sucker was already
asleep. I felt too happy and keyed up to get in a comfortable position and I was awake thinking about
Maybelle a long time. Then I dreamed about her and
it seemed I kissed her. It was a surprise to wake up
and see the dark. I lay still and a little while passed before I could come to and understand where I was.
The house was quiet and it was a very dark night.

Sucker's voice was a shock to me. "Pete? . . ."

I didn't answer anything or even move.

"You do like me as much as if I was your own
brother, don't you Pete?"

I couldn't get over the surprise of everything and
it was like this was the real dream instead of the other.

"You have liked me all the time like I was your own
brother, haven't you?"

"Sure," I said.

Then I got up for a few minutes. It was cold and
I was glad to come back to bed. Sucker hung on to
my back. He felt little and warm and I could feel his
warm breathing on my shoulder.

"No matter what you did I always knew you liked
me."

I was wide awake and my mind seemed mixed up
in a strange way. There was this happiness about
Maybelle and all that—but at the same time something
about Sucker and his voice when he said these things
made me take notice. Anyway I guess you understand
people better when you are happy than when something is worrying you. It was like I had never really
thought about Sucker until then. I felt I had always
been mean to him. One night a few weeks before I

had heard him crying in the dark. He said he had lost a boy's beebee gun and was scared to let anybody know. He wanted me to tell him what to do. I was sleepy and tried to make him hush and when he wouldn't I kicked at him. That was just one of the things I remembered. It seemed to me he had always been a lonesome kid. I felt bad.

There is something about a dark cold night that makes you feel close to someone you're sleeping with. When you talk together it is like you are the only people awake in the town.

"You're a swell kid, Sucker," I said.

It seemed to me suddenly that I did like him more than anybody else I knew—more than any other boy, more than my sisters, more in a certain way even than Maybelle. I felt good all over and it was like when they play sad music in the movies. I wanted to show Sucker how much I really thought of him and make up for the way I had always treated him.

We talked for a good while that night. His voice was fast and it was like he had been saving up these things to tell me for a long time. He mentioned that he was going to try to build a canoe and that the kids down the block wouldn't let him in on their football team and I don't know what all. I talked some too and it was a good feeling to think of him taking in everything I said so seriously. I even spoke of Maybelle a little, only I made out like it was her who had been running after me all this time. He asked questions about high school and so forth. His voice was excited and he kept on talking fast like he could never get the words out in time. When I went to sleep he was still talking and I could still feel his breathing on my shoulder, warm and close.

During the next couple of weeks I saw a lot of Maybelle. She acted as though she really cared for me a little. Half the time I felt so good I hardly knew what to do with myself.

But I didn't forget about Sucker. There were a lot of old things in my bureau drawer I'd been saving—boxing gloves and Tom Swift books and second rate fishing tackle. All this I turned over to him. We had some more talks together and it was really like I was knowing him for the first time. When there was a long cut on his cheek I knew he had been monkeying around with this new first razor set of mine, but I didn't say anything. His face seemed different now. He used to look timid and sort of like he was afraid of a whack over the head. That expression was gone. His face, with those wide-open eyes and his ears sticking out and his mouth never quite shut, had the look of a person who is surprised and expecting something swell.

Once I started to point him out to Maybelle and tell her he was my kid brother. It was an afternoon when a murder mystery was on at the movie. I had earned a dollar working for my Dad and I gave Sucker a quarter to go and get candy and so forth. With the rest I took Maybelle. We were sitting near the back and I saw Sucker come in. He began to stare at the screen the minute he stepped past the ticket man and he stumbled down the aisle without noticing where he was going. I started to punch Maybelle but couldn't quite make up my mind. Sucker looked a little silly—walking like a drunk with his eyes glued to the movie. He was wiping his reading glasses on his shirt tail and his knickers flopped down. He went on until he got to the first few rows where the kids usually sit. I never did punch Maybelle. But I got to thinking it was good to have both of them at the movie with the money I earned.

I guess things went on like this for about a month or six weeks. I felt so good I couldn't settle down to study or put my mind on anything. I wanted to be friendly with everybody. There were times when I just had to talk to some person. And usually that would be Sucker. He felt as good as I did. Once he said: "Pete, I am gladder that you are like my brother than anything else in the world."

Then something happened between Maybelle and me. I never have figured out just what it was. Girls like her are hard to understand. She began to act different toward me. At first I wouldn't let myself believe this and tried to think it was just my imagination. She didn't act glad to see me any more. Often she went out riding with this fellow on the football team who owns this yellow roadster. The car was the color of her hair and after school she would ride off with him, laughing and looking into his face. I couldn't think of anything to do about it and she was on my mind all day and night. When I did get a chance to go out with her she was snippy and didn't seem to notice me. This made me feel like something was the matter—I would worry about my shoes clopping too loud on the floor, or the fly of my pants, or the bumps on my chin. Sometimes when Maybelle was around, a devil would get into me and I'd hold my face stiff and call grown men by their last names without the Mister and say rough things. In the night I would wonder what made me do all this until I was too tired for sleep.

At first I was so worried I just forgot about Sucker. Then later he began to get on my nerves. He was always hanging around until I would get back from high school, always looking like he had something to say to me or wanted me to tell him. He made me a magazine rack in his Manual Training class and one week he saved his lunch money and bought me three packs of cigarettes. He couldn't seem to take it in that I had things on my mind and didn't want to fool with him. Every afternoon it would be the same —him in my room with this waiting expression on his face. Then I wouldn't say anything or I'd maybe answer him rough-like and he would finally go on out.

I can't divide that time up and say this happened one day and that the next. For one thing I was so mixed up the weeks just slid along into each other and I felt like Hell and didn't care. Nothing definite was said or done. Maybelle still rode around with this fellow in his yellow roadster and sometimes she would smile at me and sometimes not. Every afternoon I went from one place to another where I thought she would be. Either she would act almost nice and I would begin thinking how things would finally clear up and she would care for me—or else she'd behave so that if she hadn't been a girl I'd have wanted to grab her by that white little neck and choke her. The more ashamed I felt for making a fool of myself the more I ran after her.

Sucker kept getting on my nerves more and more. He would look at me as though he sort of blamed me for something, but at the same time knew that it wouldn't last long. He was growing fast and for some reason began to stutter when he talked. Sometimes he had nightmares or would throw up his breakfast. Mom got him a bottle of cod liver oil.

Then the finish came between Maybelle and me. I met her going to the drug store and asked for a date. When she said no I remarked something sarcastic. She told me she was sick and tired of my being around and that she had never cared a rap about me. She said all that. I just stood there and didn't answer anything. I walked home very slowly.

For several afternoons I stayed in my room by myself. I didn't want to go anywhere or talk to anyone. When Sucker would come in and look at me sort of funny I'd yell at him to get out. I didn't want to think of Maybelle and I sat at my desk reading *Popular Mechanics* or whittling at a toothbrush rack I was making. It seemed to me I was putting that girl out of my mind pretty well.

But you can't help what happens to you at night. That is what made things how they are now.

You see a few nights after Maybelle said those words to me I dreamed about her again. It was like that first time and I was squeezing Sucker's arm so tight I woke him up. He reached for my hand.

"Pete, what's the matter with you?"

All of a sudden I felt so mad my throat choked—at myself and the dream and Maybelle and Sucker and every single person I knew. I remembered all the times Maybelle had humiliated me and everything bad that had ever happened. It seemed to me for a second that nobody would ever like me but a sap like Sucker.

"Why is it we aren't buddies like we were before? Why—?"

"Shut your damn trap!" I threw off the cover and got up and turned on the light. He sat in the middle of the bed, his eyes blinking and scared.

There was something in me and I couldn't help myself. I don't think anybody ever gets that mad but once. Words came without me knowing what they would be. It was only afterward that I could remember each thing I said and see it all in a clear way.

"Why aren't we buddies? Because you're the dumbest slob I ever saw! Nobody cares anything about you! And just because I felt sorry for you sometimes and tried to act decent don't think I give a damn about a dumb-bunny like you!"

If I'd talked loud or hit him it wouldn't have been so bad. But my voice was slow and like I was very calm. Sucker's mouth was part way open and he looked as though he'd knocked his funny bone. His face was white and sweat came out on his forehead. He wiped it away with the back of his hand and for a minute his arm stayed raised that way as though he was holding something away from him.

"Don't you know a single thing? Haven't you ever been around at all? Why don't you get a girl friend instead of me? What kind of a sissy do you want to grow up to be anyway?"

I didn't know what was coming next. I couldn't help myself or think.

Sucker didn't move. He had on one of my pajama jackets and his neck stuck out skinny and small. His hair was damp on his forehead.

"Why do you always hang around me? Don't you know when you're not wanted?"

Afterward I could remember the change in Sucker's face. Slowly that blank look went away and he closed his mouth. His eyes got narrow and his fists shut. There had never been such a look on him before. It was like every second he was getting older. There was a hard look to his eyes you don't see usually in a kid. A drop of sweat rolled down his chin and he didn't notice. He just sat there with those eyes on me and he didn't speak and his face was hard and didn't move.

"No you don't know when you're not wanted. You're too dumb. Just like your name—a dumb Sucker."

It was like something had busted inside me. I turned off the light and sat down in the chair by the window. My legs were shaking and I was so tired I could have bawled. The room was cold and dark. I sat there for a long time and smoked a squashed cigarette I had saved. Outside the yard was black and quiet. After a while I heard Sucker lie down.

I wasn't mad any more, only tired. It seemed awful to me that I had talked like that to a kid only twelve. I couldn't take it all in. I told myself I would go over to him and try to make it up. But I just sat there in the cold until a long time had passed. I planned how I could straighten it out in the morning. Then, trying not to squeak the springs, I got back in bed.

Sucker was gone when I woke up the next day. And later when I wanted to apologize as I had planned he looked at me in this new hard way so that I couldn't say a word.

All of that was two or three months ago. Since then Sucker has grown faster than any boy I ever saw. He's almost as tall as I am and his bones have gotten heavier and bigger. He won't wear any of my old clothes any more and has bought his first pair of long pants—with some leather suspenders to hold them up. Those are just the changes that are easy to see and put into words.

Our room isn't mine at all any more. He's gotten up this gang of kids and they have a club. When they aren't digging trenches in some vacant lot and fighting they are always in my room. On the door there is some foolishness written in Mercurochrome saying "Woe to the Outsider who Enters" and signed with crossed bones and their secret initials. They have rigged up a radio and every afternoon it blares out music. Once as I was coming in I heard a boy telling something in a low voice about what he saw in the back of his big brother's automobile. I could guess what I didn't hear. *That's what her and my brother do. It's the truth—parked in the car.* For a minute Sucker looked surprised and his face was almost like it used to be. Then he got hard and tough again. "Sure, dumbell. We know all that." They didn't notice me. Sucker began telling them how in two years he was planning to be a trapper in Alaska.

But most of the time Sucker stays by himself. It is worse when we are alone together in the room. He sprawls across the bed in those long corduroy pants with the suspenders and just stares at me with that hard, half sneering look. I fiddle around my desk and can't get settled because of those eyes of his. And the thing is I just have to study because I've gotten three bad cards this term already. If I flunk English I can't graduate next year. I don't want to be a bum and I just have to get my mind on it. I don't care a flip for Maybelle or any particular girl any more and it's only this thing between Sucker and me that is the trouble now. We never speak except when we have to before the family. I don't even want to call him Sucker any more and unless I forget I call him by his real name, Richard. At night I can't study with him in the room and I have to hang around the drug store, smoking and doing nothing, with the fellows who loaf there.

More than anything I want to be easy in my mind again. And I miss the way Sucker and I were for a while in a funny, sad way that before this I never would have believed. But everything is so different that there seems to be nothing I can do to get it right. I've sometimes thought if we could have it out in a big fight that would help. But I can't fight him because he's four years younger. And another thing—sometimes this look in his eyes makes me almost believe that if Sucker could he would kill me.

Antaeus

BY BORDEN DEAL

THIS WAS during the wartime, when lots of people were coming North for jobs in factories and war industries, when people moved around a lot more than they do now and sometimes kids were thrown into new groups and new lives that were completely different from anything they had ever known before. I remember this one kid; T. J. his name was, from somewhere down South, whose family moved into our building during that time. They'd come North with everything they owned piled into the back seat of an old-model sedan that you wouldn't expect could make the trip, with T. J. and his three younger sisters riding shakily atop the load of junk.

Our building was just like all the others there, with families crowded into a few rooms, and I guess there were twenty-five or thirty kids about my age in that one building. Of course, there were a few of us who formed a gang and ran together all the time after school, and I was the one who brought T. J. in and started the whole thing.

The building right next door to us was a factory where they made walking dolls. It was a low building with a flat, tarred roof that had a parapet all around it about head-high and we'd found out a long time before that no one, not even the watchman, paid any attention to the roof because it was higher than any of the other buildings around. So my gang used the roof as a headquarters. We could get up there by crossing over to the fire escape from our own roof on a plank and then going on up. It was a secret place

for us, where nobody else could go without our permission.

I remember the day I first took T. J. up there to
meet the gang. He was a stocky, robust kid with a
shock of white hair, nothing sissy about him except
his voice—he talked different from any of us and you
noticed it right away. But I liked him anyway, so I
told him to come on up.

We climbed up over the parapet and dropped down
on the roof. The rest of the gang were already there.

"Hi," I said. I jerked my thumb at T. J. "He just
moved into the building yesterday."

He just stood there, not scared or anything, just
looking, like the first time you see somebody you're
not sure you're going to like.

"Hi," Blackie said. "Where you from?"

"Marion County," T. J. said.

We laughed. "Marion County?" I said. "Where's
that?"

He looked at me like I was a stranger, too. "It's in
Alabama," he said, like I ought to know where it was.

"What's your name?" Charley said.

"T. J.," he said, looking back at him. He had pale
blue eyes that looked washed-out but he looked directly at Charley, waiting for his reaction. He'll be
all right, I thought. No sissy in him . . . except that
voice. Who ever talked like that?

"T. J.," Blackie said. "That's just initials. What's
your real name? Nobody in the world has just
initials."

"I do," he said. "And they're T. J. That's all the
name I got."

His voice was resolute with the knowledge of his
rightness and for a moment no one had anything to
say. T. J. looked around at the rooftop and down at
the black tar under his feet. "Down yonder where I
come from," he said, "we played out in the woods.
Don't you-all have no woods around here?"

"Naw," Blackie said. "There's the park a few blocks
over, but it's full of kids and cops and old women.
You can't do a thing."

T. J. kept looking at the tar under his feet. "You mean you ain't got no fields to raise nothing in? No watermelons or nothing?"

"Naw," I said scornfully. "What do you want to grow something for? The folks can buy everything they need at the store."

He looked at me again with that strange, unknowing look. "In Marion County," he said, "I had my own acre of cotton and my own acre of corn. It was mine to plant ever' year."

He sounded like it was something to be proud of, and in some obscure way it made the rest of us angry. "Heck!" Blackie said. "Who'd want to have their own acre of cotton and corn? That's just work. What can you do with an acre of cotton and corn?"

T. J. looked at him. "Well, you get part of the bale offen your acre," he said seriously. "And I fed my acre of corn to my calf."

We didn't really know what he was talking about, so we were more puzzled than angry; otherwise, I guess, we'd have chased him off the roof and wouldn't let him be part of our gang. But he was strange and different and we were all attracted by his stolid sense of rightness and belonging, maybe by the strange softness of his voice contrasting our own tones of speech into harshness.

He moved his foot against the black tar. "We could make our own field right here," he said softly, thoughtfully. "Come spring we could raise us what we want to . . . watermelons and garden truck and no telling what all."

"You'd have to be a good farmer to make these tar roofs grow any watermelons," I said. We all laughed.

But T. J. looked serious. "We could haul us some dirt up here," he said. "And spread it out even and water it and before you know it we'd have us a crop in here." He looked at us intently. "Wouldn't that be fun?"

"They wouldn't let us," Blackie said quickly.

"I thought you said this was you-all's roof," T. J.

said to me. "That you-all could do anything you wanted up here."

"They've never bothered us," I said. I felt the idea beginning to catch fire in me. It was a big idea and it took a while for it to sink in but the more I thought about it the better I liked it. "Say," I said to the gang, "he might have something there. Just make us a regular roof garden, with flowers and grass and trees and everything. And all ours, too," I said. "We wouldn't let anybody up here except the ones we wanted to."

"It'd take a while to grow trees," T. J. said quickly, but we weren't paying any attention to him. They were all talking about it suddenly, all excited with the idea after I'd put it in a way they could catch hold of it. Only rich people had roof gardens, we knew, and the idea of our own private domain excited them.

"We could bring it up in sacks and boxes," Blackie said. "We'd have to do it while the folks weren't paying any attention to us. We'd have to come up to the roof of our building and then cross over with it."

"Where could we get the dirt?" somebody said worriedly.

"Out of those vacant lots over close to school," Blackie said. "Nobody'd notice if we scraped it up."

I slapped T. J. on the shoulder. "Man, you had a wonderful idea," I said, and everybody grinned at him, remembering he had started it. "Our own private roof garden."

He grinned back. "It'll be ourn," he said. "All ourn." Then he looked thoughtful again. "Maybe I can lay my hands on some cotton seed, too. You think we could raise us some cotton?"

We'd started big projects before at one time or another, like any gang of kids, but they'd always petered out for lack of organization and direction. But this one didn't . . . somehow or other T. J. kept it going all through the winter months. He kept talking about the watermelons and the cotton we'd raise, come spring, and when even that wouldn't work he'd switch around to my idea of flowers and grass and trees though he was always honest enough to add that it'd take a while to get any trees started. He always had it on his mind and he'd mention it in school, getting them lined up to carry dirt that afternoon, saying in a casual way that he reckoned a few more weeks ought to see the job through.

Our little area of private earth grew slowly. T. J. was smart enough to start in one corner of the building, heaping up the carried earth two or three feet thick, so that we had an immediate result to look at, to contemplate with awe. Some of the evenings T. J. alone was carrying earth up to the building, the rest of the gang distracted by other enterprises or interests, but T. J. kept plugging along on his own and eventually we'd all come back to him again and then our own little acre would grow more rapidly.

He was careful about the kind of dirt he'd let us carry up there and more than once he dumped a sandy load over the parapet into the areaway below because it wasn't good enough. He found out the kinds of earth in all the vacant lots for blocks around. He'd pick it up and feel it and smell it, frozen though it was sometimes, and then he'd say it was good growing soil or it wasn't worth anything and we'd have to go on somewhere else.

Thinking about it now I don't see how he kept us at it. It was hard work, lugging paper sacks and boxes of dirt all the way up the stairs of our own building, keeping out of the way of the grownups so they wouldn't catch on to what we were doing. They probably wouldn't have cared, for they didn't pay much attention to us, but we wanted to keep it secret anyway. Then we had to go through the trap door to our roof, teeter over a plank to the fire escape, then climb two or three stories to the parapet and drop down onto the roof. All that for a small pile of earth that sometimes didn't seem worth the effort. But T. J. kept the vision bright within us, his words shrewd and calculated toward the fulfillment of his dream; and he worked harder than any of us. He seemed driven toward a goal that we couldn't see, a particular point in time that would be definitely marked by signs and wonders that only he could see.

The laborious earth just lay there during the cold months, inert and lifeless, the clods lumpy and cold under our feet when we walked over it. But one day it rained and afterward there was a softness in the air and the earth was alive and giving again with moisture and warmth. That evening T. J. smelled the air, his nostrils dilating with the odor of the earth under his feet.

"It's spring," he said, and there was a gladness rising in his voice that filled us all with the same feeling. "It's mighty late for it, but it's spring. I'd just about decided it wasn't never gonna get here at all."

We were all sniffing at the air, too, trying to smell it the way that T. J. did, and I can still remember the sweet odor of the earth under our feet. It was the first time in my life that spring and spring earth had meant anything to me. I looked at T. J. then, knowing in a faint way the hunger within him through the toilsome winter months, knowing the dream that lay behind his plan. He was a new Antaeus, preparing his own bed of strength.

"Planting time," he said. "We'll have to find us some seed."

"What do we do?" Blackie said. "How do we do it?"

"First we'll have to break up the clods," T. J. said. "That won't be hard to do. Then we plant the seed and after a while they come up. Then you got you a crop." He frowned. "But you ain't got it raised yet. You got to tend it and hoe it and take care of it and all the time it's growing and growing while you're awake and while you're asleep. Then you lay it by when it's growed and let it ripen and then you got you a crop."

"There's those wholesale seed houses over on Sixth," I said. "We could probably swipe some grass seed over there."

T. J. looked at the earth. "You-all seem mighty set

on raising some grass," he said. "I ain't never put no effort into that. I spent all my life trying not to raise grass."

"But it's pretty," Blackie said. "We could play on it and take sunbaths on it. Like having our own lawn. Lots of people got lawns."

"Well," T. J. said. He looked at the rest of us, hesitant for the first time. He kept on looking at us for a moment. "I did have it in mind to raise some corn and vegetables. But we'll plant grass."

He was smart. He knew where to give in. And I don't suppose it made any difference to him really. He just wanted to grow something, even if it was grass.

"Of course," he said, "I do think we ought to plant a row of watermelons. They'd be mighty nice to eat while we was a-laying on that grass."

We all laughed. "All right," I said. "We'll plant us a row of watermelons."

Things went very quickly then. Perhaps half the roof was covered with the earth, the half that wasn't broken by ventilators, and we swiped pocketfuls of grass seed from the open bins in the wholesale seed house, mingling among the buyers on Saturdays and during the school lunch hour. T. J. showed us how to prepare the earth, breaking up the clods and smoothing it and sowing the grass seed. It looked rich and black now with moisture, receiving of the seed, and it seemed that the grass sprang up overnight, pale green in the early spring.

We couldn't keep from looking at it, unable to believe that we had created this delicate growth. We looked at T. J. with understanding now, knowing the fulfillment of the plan he had carried alone within his mind. We had worked without full understanding of the task but he had known all the time.

We found that we couldn't walk or play on the delicate blades, as we had expected to, but we didn't mind. It was enough just to look at it, to realize that it was the work of our own hands, and each evening the whole gang was there, trying to measure the growth that had been achieved that day.

One time a foot was placed on the plot of ground . . . one time only Blackie stepping onto it with sudden bravado. Then he looked at the crushed blades and there was shame in his face. He did not do it again. This was his grass, too, and not to be desecrated. No one said anything, for it was not necessary.

T. J. had reserved a small section for watermelons and he was still trying to find some seed for it. The wholesale house didn't have any watermelon seed and we didn't know where we could lay our hands on them. T. J. shaped the earth into mounds, ready to receive them, three mounds lying in a straight line along the edge of the grass plot.

We had just about decided that we'd have to buy the seed if we were to get them. It was a violation of our principles but we were anxious to get the watermelons started. Somewhere or other, T. J. got his hands on a seed catalogue and brought it one evening to our roof garden.

"We can order them now," he said, showing us the catalogue. "Look!"

We all crowded around, looking at the fat, green watermelons pictured in full color on the pages. Some of them were split open, showing the red, tempting meat, making our mouths water.

"Now we got to scrape up some seed money," T. J. said, looking at us. "I got a quarter. How much you-all got?"

We made up a couple of dollars between us and T. J. nodded his head. "That'll be more than enough. Now we got to decide what kind to get. I think them Kleckley Sweets. What do you-all think?"

He was going into esoteric matters beyond our reach. We hadn't even known there were different kinds of melons. So we just nodded our heads and agreed that yes, we thought the Kleckley Sweets, too.

"I'll order them tonight," T. J. said. "We ought to have them in a few days."

Then an adult voice said behind us: "What are you boys doing up here?"

It startled us for no one had ever come up here before, in all the time we had been using the roof of the factory. We jerked around and saw three men standing near the trap door at the other end of the roof. They weren't policemen, or night watchmen, but three men in plump business suits, looking at us. They walked toward us.

"What are you boys doing up here?" the one in the middle said again.

We stood still, guilt heavy among us, levied by the tone of voice, and looked at the three strangers.

The men stared at the grass flourishing behind us. "What's this?" the man said. "How did this get up here?"

"Sure is growing good, ain't it?" T. J. said conversationally. "We planted it."

The men kept looking at the grass as if they didn't believe it. It was a thick carpet over the earth now, a patch of deep greenness startling in the sterile industrial surroundings.

"Yes, sir," T. J. said proudly. "We toted that earth up here and planted that grass." He fluttered the seed catalogue. "And we're just fixing to plant us some watermelon."

The man looked at him then, his eyes strange and faraway. "What do you mean, putting this on the roof of my building?" he said. "Do you want to go to jail?"

T. J. looked shaken. The rest of us were silent, frightened by the authority of his voice. We had grown up aware of adult authority, of policemen and night watchmen and teachers, and this man sounded like all the others. But it was a new thing to T. J.

"Well, you wan't using the roof," T. J. said. He paused a moment and added shrewdly, "So we just thought to pretty it up a little bit."

"And sag it so I'd have to rebuild it," the man said sharply. He turned away, saying to a man beside him, "See that all that junk is shoveled off by tomorrow."

"Yes, sir," the man said.

T. J. started forward. "You can't do that," he said.

"We toted it up here and it's our earth. We planted it and raised it and toted it up here."

The man stared at him coldly. "But it's my building," he said. "It's to be shoveled off tomorrow."

"It's our earth," T. J. said desperately. "You ain't got no right!"

The men walked on without listening and descended clumsily through the trap door. T. J. stood looking after them, his body tense with anger, until they had disappeared. They wouldn't even argue with him, wouldn't let him defend his earth-rights.

He turned to us. "We won't let 'em do it," he said fiercely. "We'll stay up here all day tomorrow and the day after that and we won't let 'em do it."

We just looked at him. We knew that there was no stopping it. He saw it in our faces and his face wavered for a moment before he gripped it into determination.

"They ain't got no right," he said. "It's our earth. It's our land. Can't nobody touch a man's own land."

We kept on looking at him, listening to the words but knowing that it was no use. The adult world had descended on us even in our richest dream and we knew there was no calculating the adult world, no fighting it, no winning against it.

We started moving slowly toward the parapet and the fire escape, avoiding a last look at the green beauty of the earth that T. J. had planted for us . . . had planted deeply in our minds as well as in our experience. We filed slowly over the edge and down the steps to the plank, T. J. coming last, and all of us could feel the weight of his grief behind us.

"Wait a minute," he said suddenly, his voice harsh with the effort of calling. We stopped and turned, held by the tone of his voice, and looked up at him standing above us on the fire escape.

"We can't stop them?" he said, looking down at us, his face strange in the dusky light. "There ain't no way to stop 'em?"

"No," Blackie said with finality. "They own the building."

We stood still for a moment, looking up at T. J., caught into inaction by the decision working in his face. He stared back at us and his face was pale and mean in the poor light, with a bald nakedness in his skin like cripples have sometimes.

"They ain't gonna touch my earth," he said fiercely. "They ain't gonna lay a hand on it! Come on."

He turned around and started up the fire escape again, almost running against the effort of climbing. We followed more slowly, not knowing what he intended. By the time we reached him, he had seized a board and thrust it into the soil, scooping it up and flinging it over the parapet into the areaway below. He straightened and looked us squarely in the face.

"They can't touch it," he said. "I won't let 'em lay a dirty hand on it!"

We saw it then. He stooped to his labor again and we followed, the gusts of his anger moving in frenzied labor among us as we scattered along the edge of earth, scooping it and throwing it over the parapet, destroying with anger the growth we had nurtured with such tender care. The soil carried so laboriously upward to the light and the sun cascaded swiftly into the dark areaway, the green blades of grass crumpled and twisted in the falling.

It took less time than you would think . . . the task of destruction is infinitely easier than that of creation. We stopped at the end, leaving only a scattering of loose soil, and when it was finally over a stillness stood among the group and over the factory building. We looked down at the bare sterility of black tar, felt the harsh texture of it under the soles of our shoes, and the anger had gone out of us, leaving only a sore aching in our minds like over-stretched muscles.

T. J. stooped for a moment, his breathing slowing from anger and effort, caught into the same contemplation of destruction as all of us. He stooped slowly, finally, and picked up a lonely blade of grass left trampled under our feet and put it between his teeth tasting it, sucking the greenness out of it into his mouth. Then he started walking toward the fire escape, moving before any of us were ready to move, and disappeared over the edge while we stared after him.

We followed him but he was already halfway down to the ground, going on past the board where we crossed over, climbing down into the areaway. We saw the last section swing down with his weight and then he stood on the concrete below us, looking at the small pile of anonymous earth scattered by our throwing. Then he walked across the place where we could see him and disappeared toward the street without glancing back, without looking up to see us watching him.

They did not find him for two weeks. Then the Nashville police caught him just outside the Nashville freight yards. He was walking along the railroad track; still heading south, still heading home.

As for us, who had no remembered home to call us . . . none of us ever again climbed the escape-way to the roof.

A Field of Rice

BY PEARL S. BUCK

WANG SAN, the head man in the village of San-li-wan-tse, listened to the young man with attention. He was an earnest young man, even a good young man, but his ignorance was to be pitied. Most pitiable of all was the evidence that he was too ignorant to know that he was ignorant. But he must be heard since he had been sent down from those above, in Peking, and everyone knows it is best to listen to them, and if possible, without reply. So far Wang San had restrained himself. He had said nothing. Now however, standing here on the village threshing floor, surrounded by his silent neighbors, he felt an irrepressible determination rising inside his breast, a recklessness which amounted to desperation. It was all very well to listen when the talk was of how fine a man Chairman Mao was and how wicked were the American imperialists. He had never seen Chairman Mao nor had he ever seen an American. But rice he knew. Yes, he knew all about rice, the garnering of the special seed, its planting in the narrow seed beds of rich earth, the transplanting into the watery fields, and at last reaping of the harvest. No one could tell him anything about rice. He raised his voice.

"Comrade Li!"

The young man stopped talking to look about for the voice.

"It is I," Wang San said. He pushed his way among the crowd of country folk.

"What do you wish to say?" Comrade Li asked.

Wang San stood with his legs apart and his arms

folded across his breast. His blue cotton jacket and trousers were clean but patched in many places. One suit a year of blue cotton was all that could be expected nowadays and last year's suit went to patch this year's. Even so, one suit is not enough. There was talk of two suits as a necessity. In old times, when every man was responsible for his own clothes, it was easy enough to have several suits at a time. One could then think only of himself and his family. In these new times this was no longer possible. If a man asked for two suits a year, it meant millions of suits, for if he had two suits, all other men must have two, not to mention women and children. It was impossible.

Wang Lung replied to Comrade Li in his usual loud clear voice. "I wish to say that this new way of planting rice will ruin our fields."

Comrade Li was a thin tall young man. He had a long thin face and his lips and eyes were narrow. "Comrade Wang," he said coldly, "is it possible that you believe you know more than our Chairman Mao?"

Wang Lung felt a strong pull on the tail of his jacket. He recognized the tug of his wife's admonishing hand. She had followed him then! Be quiet, she was trying to tell him. Remember that our village elders were shot for less than this! He did not heed her. They could live without the village elders, but not without rice. He let his arms drop to his sides. He made his voice gentle and reasonable, but he went on.

"Comrade Li, there are many things that Chairman Mao knows which I do not know. But rice is our livelihood and perhaps it is not his. He is gentlefolk and I am not. His father was a landowner, but mine was a farmer. And my grandfather was a farmer and my ancestral fathers before that. These fields have been planted to rice for thousands of years. And not just to any rice, either, but to the special rice which grows best in our earth here, under our feet."

He stamped his right foot on the earth. Comrade Li was listening, his mouth curved in a thin downward smile.

"Go on, Comrade Wang," he said with ostentatious patience.

He had been taught that he must be patient with these land folk, but never lenient. Let them talk and show their hearts. Then let unrelenting judgment be made. The crowd stood in silence, their eyes downcast. A woman's wail broke the silence. It was Wang San's wife. She had turned and run through the crowd back to the small earthen house where they still lived. There was the sound of a wooden door slammed and a bar drawn across it.

"Go on, Comrade Wang," Comrade Li said again.

So Wang San went on, although now a chill of fear crept out of his heart. He wet his lips.

"You say the Americans plough their fields deeply and they get great harvests. You say they have machines that plough and now Chairman Mao has bought such machines from our Russian brothers. With these machines you tell us we must now plough our fields deeply. But the question is, do the Americans plant rice in their deeply ploughed fields? The question is—"

Comrade Li's patience suddenly broke. "The question is whether you, Wang San, will do as you are told. I will answer this question for you. You will do as you are told. All of you will do as you are told. You are ignorant men. You cannot even write your names. You cannot read instructions. Therefore I have come here to your small village to tell you what you cannot read. The whole region, from Wan-li-hsiang to San-li-wan-tse is to be one great field of rice. All boundaries are to be removed and the work will be done by the whole commune. You will be allowed for the present to live in your own houses, but the land is no longer yours. It belongs to all. You will receive instructions from men trained abroad in agriculture. We can no longer leave our precious soil in the hands of ignorant men. Is your question answered, Comrade Wang?"

Wang San stared into the narrow eyes. In his mind uncertainty mingled with fear. Perhaps the young man

was right. This deep ploughing had never been tried.
There might be virtue in it. Yet had not his own father told him that rice fields were never to be
ploughed too deeply? No more than enough for the
roots of the rice plants to be in the water while their
heads stood above, his father said! That and the careful choice of seeds were what made a full harvest.
"Rice is as wilful as woman," his father had told him
often as they transplanted the young seedlings into
their watery beds. "Treat rice in the way it likes
best and you will never starve. Forget what it wants
and it withers without harvest. The seed must be kept
pure. Each region has its own rice. Never mix the
seed."

Remembering these words of his father, Wang San
was about to urge them upon Comrade Li. He might
have done so had not the villagers grown afraid.
They gathered around him and hustled him away,
crying out in various voices, none wishing to tell his
name, that Wang San would obey and they would
all obey. Only let Comrade Li continue his instructions and they would be carried out.

So Comrade Li continued. "The new plows will
arrive on time. With them will come instructors to
teach you how to use them. Meanwhile you must dig
up the paths between the fields and make these petty
bits of land into one vast plain, ready to be ploughed.
You will see such harvest as you have never seen."

Wang San was now on the edge of the crowd and
still being pushed. He made one last effort to stand
his ground. "The seed," he shouted over the heads of
the crowd. "Where shall we get the seed?"

"The seed will be provided," Comrade Li shouted
back.

"But—but—" Wang San could say no more. Strong
hands pressed over his mouth and he was hurried
across the street and into the field behind the houses.

"You fool," the villagers hissed at him. "Are we
all to be killed for your sake?"

"You will starve," he muttered.

"At least it will not be tomorrow," they retorted and left him there alone.

He squatted on his heels then, his back to the houses, and stared out over the fields. It was nearly spring. The seed beds must soon be prepared and the rice planted. He had his own store of seed, hidden in a jar under the eaves of his house. Let it stay there. He would not give it to anyone. A year, two years, ten years, it would remain as it was, until some day he would plant it himself. As for Comrade Li and all such Comrades, if they would not listen to landfolk who had been farmers for thousands of years, farmers who knew the soil as they knew their own flesh, who could tell by the feel of a grain of rice whether it was the right kind of seed, then let them starve, too. Sooner or later they would learn by starvation.

Nevertheless he felt a great pity for Comrade Li as he thought of him starving. The young man was not a bad young man. On the contrary, he was good. It was simply that he was mistaken. He thought he was doing right but he was doing wrong. He had been misinformed by someone above. Sitting there in the mild sunshine of a late winter's day, in fact a day on the edge of spring, he considered Chairman Mao. Had Chairman Mao ever ploughed a field himself, following behind an ox or a water buffalo? Or had he, as the son of landed gentry, merely seen the harvests come in, heaps of rice poured into the bins of his father's storehouses, wheat filling the vats, pigs slaughtered for winter meat, cabbages salted down into the great pottery jars glazed inside to keep the vegetables sweet? It made a great difference how one had learned. As for those western peoples and their deep ploughing, who knew what they ate or what they raised? Who knew anything about them? One heard nowadays that the Americans were evil. So why deep plough the fields here if that was what the Americans did over there? Yet all this was not the fault of Comrade Li. That young man was a patriot, make no mistake. He could have sat in some comfortable

city office, but instead he was here in the country,
eating plain food and sleeping on boards, enduring
the cold and the stink of the village in order to serve
his country, or so he thought. It was certain, however, that he knew nothing about farming.

While he meditated Wang San decided to make one
more effort. He would wait until night and then,
while the village slept, he would seek out Comrade
Li in his small room in the school master's poor house,
and reason with him, alone and with no villager to
spoil the argument. That night, then, while Comrade
Li sat by the wooden table in his room, writing his
report of the day's work, Wang San coughed outside
the open door. Comrade Li looked up.

"Well?" he said curtly.

"You are very busy," Wang San said politely.

"I am always busy," Comrade Li replied. "What
is it you want?"

Wang San edged into the room. It was a small room
and he felt too big. He laughed unhappily and
scratched his head.

"About the rice fields," he began.

Comrade Li slapped his pen down on the table.
"What about the rice fields?" he barked.

Wang San hesitated. Why had he begun with the
rice field? He should have made the usual courteous
inquiries about Comrade Li's home, his health and his
parents' health. He began again.

"Comrade Li, where is your honorable residence?"

Comrade Li stared at him. "What is that to you?"

Wang San went bravely on. "And how is your
honorable health?"

"Are you joking me?" Comrade Li asked sternly.
"Why are you here in the night asking me bourgeois
questions?"

"These questions cannot now be asked?" Wang San
inquired.

"Certainly not," Comrade Li snapped. "My home
is wherever I work. At present it is in this room. And
my health does not matter so long as I am able to do
the work required of me."

"Your parents—"

"I have no parents," Comrade Li said coldly.

"You mean—"

"Simply that I have no parents."

Wang San was horrified. How could it be possible that a man as young as Comrade Li had no parents? His own father was dead of a fever, but his old mother was still alive.

"How did they die?" he asked gently.

Comrade Li did not reply. He turned his face away and stared at the earthen wall. Wang San sighed in sympathy. "I know how you feel, Comrade Li. A man without parents is a tree without roots. And you are so young to be an orphan! You work too hard. You are very thin and pale. You are grieving for your parents."

Comrade Li refused comfort. "I am not grieving," he muttered. "It was not my fault that they—it was nothing that I—they were given the chance to—"

Wang San was all but overwhelmed. He had seen something of life as it was now lived. "You mean they—"

When he paused, Comrade Li turned on him. "My father was an absentee landowner. We lived in the city. We were rich. He would not reform. He would not confess. He would do nothing to change. He only laughed. He said he did not want to live. Very well then—he died. And my mother—hung herself."

Wang San was stricken. "What sorrow, what sorrow!" he groaned.

"I tell you, he brought it on himself," Comrade Li retorted with sudden violence. "It was not necessary for them to die. They—it was cruel of them not to think of me, their son. I explained to them. I begged them. I got down on my—my knees. It makes me ashamed to think of that."

"Do not be ashamed," Wang San said. "It was correct of you to beg your parents on your knees."

"It was not correct," Comrade Li shouted. "It was bourgeois! I atoned for it. I went to the—I told the authorities. I denounced my father. They came and got him."

"Prison?" Wang San asked.

"No," Comrade Li said. "It was all over in a few minutes. A trial in our own house—and—and he was shot in the courtyard."

"No wonder you are so thin," Wang said, mourning. "You cannot eat. You are always thinking of him."

"You are wrong," Comrade Li snapped. "I never think of him. What happened was right. I did my duty. Now go away and leave me to continue doing my duty."

It occurred to Wang San that he had not accomplished what he came to do. He began again.

"About the rice field—"

He was astonished to see what these few words could do. Comrade Li leaped to his feet, he made his hands into fists, and he rushed at Wang San. "Do you want to be shot out there on the threshing floor?" His voice was a bellow, so loud that it cracked as he continued. "One word from me, you dog, and they'll stand you against the wall, too! You are my responsibility. It is my duty to see that you obey orders —my duty—my duty—"

Wang San fled into the darkness. He could do no more. It was all too clear that Comrade Li could not be changed. And, as he had said, he was doing his duty. This matter of duty was dangerous. A man could commit any crime if he thought it was his duty. Yes, Comrade Li was at heart a good young man, a patriot in these new times. He was doing his best. It was entirely possible that he was doing his best even when he betrayed his father. It all depended upon what one was taught was his duty. Duty—a dangerous word! It could fall upon a man like a heavy sword and put an end to him. It could drive him into madness, he thinking all the time that he was right and others were wrong. As, for example, the matter of deep ploughing in the rice fields—Wang San shook his head, he sighed and gave up his spirit. There was no one now to whom he could protest. Even the gods were gone. The temple was empty of gods. Instead it was filled with soldiers.

Thereafter no one could have discerned the slightest difference between Wang San and his fellow villagers. Every morning they rose at dawn and marched out to the land and began the work of destroying the boundaries between the fields. Hoe and spade, they worked without rest, Comrade Li driving them on, the soldiers behind him.

"All right be ready for the transplanting of the rice," Comrade Li shouted at them.

The seed beds were doing well enough. Rice was planted early, thanks to the early spring, and the beds were well fertilized not only with manure but with foreign fertilizer as well. True, the seed was mixed. That is to say, it was not pure. All the local seed was used, but to it had been added seed from other parts of the country, for nowadays the seed was kept all together in great storage bins at central places. Any seed that a farmer had must be given over to the authorities. Wang San had disobeyed secretly and had given only half his seed store. He wondered how many of his fellow villagers had the same secret, but none dared to confide in any other. These were not the old days when a friend and neighbor could be trusted. It was not a matter of blame. It was a matter of torture and punishment. One lived as one could. Better to keep one's own secrets.

Enough of the local rice seed was planted however so that the seed beds looked green. Vast seed beds they were, for there was a vast field to flood for transplanting. When the boundaries were all smoothed away and the land lay flat as far as eye could see and far beyond the horizon, the foreign plows were brought in trucks. They were attached to foreign tractors and young men rode the tractors and set to work on the great field. The villagers could only stand aside and watch, their faces wondering and anxious.

"Ai ya," they groaned under their breath, "Ai ya— ai ya—"

For what was happening to the land was happening to their very flesh. This land, tended by human hands and so tended for thousands of years, was now rent and tortured by machines. The rich top soil was tossed this way and that, and beneath the top soil, the six inches of heavy clay which served as a bottom to hold the nourishing water for the young rice plants, was cut into strips this way and that. Beneath the clay was the porous subsoil.

"Never slice the skin of the earth," the old farmers told their sons, generation after generation. "The skin of the earth is like the skin of our bodies. It holds the earth together as our own skin holds our blood and bones."

Now the skin was torn and useless and the subsoil came spilling out, grey sand and pebbled stone. The villagers watched, desolation in their hearts. They knew what would happen. All would be as their forefathers had told them. But not one villager spoke a word. Even Wang San was silent. Of what use to speak now when the worst had been done?

Listlessly the villagers proceeded to fulfill orders, and none worked more doggedly than Wang San.

"Yes, Comrade Li," he said a hundred times a day until Comrade Li almost approved him. A faithful man, this village headman, one who had learned his lesson!

"Wang San, I will recommend you," he said at last.

"Thank you, Comrade Li," Wang San said, listlessly. He had given up all hope of the future. The only question was what would happen to Comrade Li when the worst was known.

Never had there been so fair a spring. Rains fell and the river swelled. When early summer came the seed beds were full and green and it was time for transplanting. In the old days the river water was turned into the fields by hand, banks of clay raised to the level to guide the exact depth of water needed for the rice. Now no hands were needed. Three heavy iron pumps were brought in by trucks and these were placed at various points by the river and from them the water spouted into the vast field. In two days the whole countryside was a lake, and the village sat on an island in the middle, connected with the mainland only by the raised road. Into this lake there now swarmed hundreds of workers. These also had been brought in by truck, and everywhere the blue-clad workers stooped to transplant the rice. When they had finished, the lake was all a delicate green with the young rice. Comrade Li was pleased and proud. He spent much time gazing over the new landscape, and he did not deign to speak to Wang San.

All might have gone well had it not been for the river. The trouble was with the river. It was too small. When the spring floods subsided it became a creek, meandering among sandbanks. The pumps coughed up the sandy water and then stopped, their inward parts clogged. All would have been well even then if the field could have held water when rain fell. In the old days each small field had been a separate bowl, the clay bottom firm under the topsoil. Rain or no rain, river or no river, the fields then remained flooded long enough for the maturing rice. When the drought of late summer came as usual the fields dried slowly until the rice no longer needed water. The roots by then were strong and they upheld the plants until they grew yellow with harvest.

Now there was no clay bottom. The earth dried long before the dry season and even the rains were not enough to keep the plants in water. As fast as the rains fell in the sixth month, the water seeped away into the loose subsoil and the river, though for a day or two it rose, could not maintain the level the rice plants needed. The water ran into the cracked earth and flowed uselessly away. Before the grain could head, the plants began to wither and droop.

What was now to be done? The villagers were mute. They shook their heads. Comrade Li forgot himself so far as to scream at the villagers.

"Why did you not tell me? Blockheads! Traitors! You are silent on purpose!"

Not one of them lifted his voice to reply. Not one

of them reminded Comrade Li that he had been told but he had not believed. Deep ploughing might be all very well for foreign lands but not for this ancestral earth. They were afraid of his anger, yet they were sorry for him. He had worked far beyond his strength, this thin young man. He had done his best. He had obeyed his superiors, believing that they knew what they were doing. The villagers had no heart to reproach him. As for those others who should be reproached, where were they? One could not see them anywhere. Here then was Comrade Li.

The day came when he too could only be silent. What was there to say? He was wrong. He could not acknowledge it but he knew it, and all the villagers knew that he knew it. It was Wang San who finally mustered courage to go to him and even he did not speak until the rice plants were dry straws on parched earth. He went to Comrade Li one evening as he had before. There Comrade Li sat as usual before his unpainted table, writing reports. He looked up when he saw Wang San.

"Well?" he inquired, but all the sharpness was gone from his voice.

Wang San coughed behind his hand. "In the old days," he said, "once in a score of years or so, the harvest also failed. It was not a matter of water, but —it happened."

For the first time in many weeks Comrade Li showed interest.

"Well?" he said again.

Wang San continued. "In such a time we had nothing to eat. We starved unless we went south to some great city."

"You cannot go to any city now," Comrade Li said. "In the cities they depend on you farmers for food. It is no longer possible for each small community to think only of itself. We must think of the total. When there is not enough food we are all hungry."

"How are the harvests elsewhere?" Wang San inquired.

"Not good," Comrade Li said shortly. "The seed was not good."

Wang San received this fresh blow. The seed! The seed gathered from every part of the country had been stored together, hopelessly mixed and mingled. But rice, his father always said, rice is as wilful as a woman. Each kind of rice must be kept pure in the seed, or there is no harvest.

"The people are hungry everywhere?"

It was a question, and Wang San knew the answer. Comrade Li did not speak.

Wang San hesitated. Did he dare? But life was worth little indeed if the rice failed. Comrade Li was writing his reports again as though no one else was there. Wang San drew in his breath and began desperately to say the one thing that should not be said, that could not be said.

"In the old days," he said, his voice hoarse in his throat—

Comrade Li looked at him, his narrow eyes full of hate. "Say nothing of the old days," he shouted.

But Wang San could not stop. Say it he must. "In the old days," he said very loud and fast, "when we had no food, the Americans sent us wheat and corn and—"

He got no further. From under his jacket Comrade Li took a small weapon, scarcely bigger than his hand. He leveled it at Wang San, his finger on the trigger. Wang San stiffened in terror, unable to move. This was the moment of death! Then, suddenly as he had lifted it, Comrade Li let his hand drop.

"Why should I kill you—" he muttered. And he placed the little weapon at his own right temple.

Before he could pull the trigger Wang San leaped forward. It was not a matter of thought. It was impulse, ages old. He snatched the weapon as it spit fire and crackled flame, and he shouted.

"Why should you kill yourself? You are Chinese, too!"

The weapon crashed to the floor and the two men stood face to face, gazing into each other's eyes.

Night of Vengeance

BY PAUL DARCY BOLES

BELOW DECKS in the second bank of rowers we knew we had been in a battle—and a storm following battle; yet that was all we knew. And who keeps count of battles? Or storms?

The life is that of an animal chained to a post. I, Voldi, must have been a useful animal. For I had lived, I had survived. By the calculations in my head —though sometimes they went wrong—I thought I had been a galley rower for almost a year.

As I say, it is hard keeping tally. At first when you are flung below and they lock the circles of iron around your wrists there is still pride. The pride of knowing your name, where you came from. The pride of remembering how a girl's face looked and the wine jars smelled and the dust of the road moved in the sunlight. When the pride begins to go a different desperation sets in. I have no words to tell of that other terror. Those who have been in the galleys know what truth I speak.

Oh, at first, like all the rest, I had cherished notions of escape. For the galley in which I served was not unusual. It was designed for fighting and that alone; as we Greeks had first designed such galleys for Salamis—and Salamis was 480 years before. It was a vessel of war, slim and long. Below it was packed with rowers. The light upper deck held the soldiery. They had their shields, their bows and arrows, their spears —they had their kind of freedom. When the engagements came, no matter how close to death and complete madness you might be in the rowing banks, there

124

was the chance, small but beautiful, of possible escape.

There were stories of such escape. The old man, the one we called the Bear—gods, he was full of stories! He sat ahead of me in my rowing bank. We were two of fifty-two men on that tier. In the mornings when the first light stole over the water and touched the dark wooden rim of the rowing port beside him I could always see first of all his shoulders, which were enormous; his long, thick hair, grizzled like a great bear's pelt; the way his huge head sat on the column of his neck. If it was a time when the drumbeats of the timekeepers in the bow had slackened to a slow pulsing count or nearly died out, we would talk a little. The timekeepers, who beat out on their heavy-skinned drums the rhythm of the strokes, were called the duumvir. I have thought that they were only men performing their given task. Yet to me it was the concentration of all evil. The very name, duumvir, is Roman; oh, yes, they had adopted our Greek ships, our ways of fighting, our certain wisdom. In the old days it was Themistocles the Athenian who had placed faith in the wooden walls of our triremes and who had magnificently defeated the Persians and all of Xerxes' might at Salamis! But now we had worse than a Persian fleet to conquer. Now we were slaves.

So, when I heard those strokes of the duumvir's mallets on their drums, my teeth would grind together as though I had already gone mad. It was not until I saw the light seeping in the port to touch the Bear's dignity—even naked, he possessed dignity; a hillman, he'd been, one of those who work their little crop even as Ulysses did in the golden days before war or our gods' wrath—that I could know the joy of remembering that I was, after all, still alive. And that there might still be freedom.

So we would manage to talk, the Bear and I, in those mornings. The old Bear would turn his head slowly, until I could see the brightness of one black eye. "Voldi," he would say in his gruff, half-croaking hillman's speech. "It was thirty-one years ago, I was thinking, Voldi, that the battle of Actium took place. Ah, Voldi, I was a young man then; as young as you are."

I would say, "I am not young. My hands are as old as yours, old man. I have held this oar so long my hands are grown to it. I have smelled filth and eaten bad bread and looked squinting into blackness so long I am as old as you are. I have forgotten what it is to be young."

He would laugh, a soft laugh yet harsh because of his cracked voice. "You are yet a child, for no aging philosopher could contain that bitterness. But, Voldi, I wish to tell you: I heard the news of Actium from a running messenger, four days after the event. How it stirred me! Antony against Octavian, you recall—using machines that had immense springs in them, mounted on huge wooden towers on the upper decks. The machines threw darts and boulders. But what impressed me most——"

"Antony lost that battle," I said with relish. "And who cares, when Roman fights Roman, what the outcome may be?"

"Yes, it is a child," he would say, nodding. "A child's answer. What impressed me most, Voldi, was the interesting number of galley slaves who escaped. The messenger said they had worked in concert, taking advantage of the confusion to tear up their benches——"

"And if they did, old man?" I would say softly. For the Bear when he spoke in this vein made my heart turn in my chest—in a galley it is not good to let yourself be excited too much; it brings on the madness. A dozen men had gone mad in the time of my slavery. As soon as their madness was accredited by the overseers—who whipped them to make sure they were not shamming—they were slain, then cut up with short-swords and flung through the sweep ports.

"It has been done, Voldi," he would say in his quiet husk of a voice. "It has been accomplished. Think on that."

Now we had been in a battle and in a storm afterward. The galley was removed from the bulk of the fleet; we'd been blown off course by the storm—I'd heard the officers shout it in the confusion. The memory of the battle, like ten battles before it, moved through my muscles. Once during the tumult I'd had the notion that in the screaming and the clamor of ship against ship we would, this time, go under. Yet we had not gone under; perhaps we'd won the battle.

It was night—what time I could not tell, though as a rule from the look of the water you could read the approximate times of night or day. In the hour of midnight the water would be a clear deep blue—unless we were near shore, or shoals, when it would change to a cold green. If there was a moon you could nearly tell by the light of it on the water—though you could seldom see the moon herself—what the hour might be. Yet now, though it was light out, I could not read the signs.

I will tell you: it was a strange night. I have never known a stranger one. Nor could I tell what had wakened me. After battle, or storm, or both, the overseers—and the officers, and the captain above them—have grace enough to let the rowers rest. It is a small rest, short and uneasy, filled, as all our sleep was filled, by the sudden moans of men whose very sleep is riddled by fear; by the slow sound of chains, shifting with tumbled human bodies; by the steady, undying sound of the Roman duumvir's drums. For when one pair of duumvir ceases, another takes over in its stead, and they do not miss a stroke. They were counting now, only, for the stern sweep—all other oars trailed silent; lifting myself a little, I could see the froth line along my oar blade.

That second of straining to see gave me another strange thought. It was of all the fish and the water animals in a night like this one; how pleasing it was for them to be free and unafraid! Just before the storm, while we were still shaking from the battle— when the overseers were inspecting us to see how many dead we had—many birds had come rushing by.

Through the groans of the dying, through the splashes as the bodies fell into the water, we below decks had heard the birds. For one instant I had seen them through the sweep port as they passed in a cloud—and then, I recalled, I had felt as now. There was something in me which went out and out to the tameless wonder of fish, sea animals and birds. Of course, they'd been merely the harbingers of storm, running before it like ships of the air rowed by their wings. Yet the feeling that remained was the same I had often from the old man called the Bear. And suddenly, as I watched, I saw that the old man also was awake, for he turned his head to me.

"Voldi," he said. There was that in his voice which had been there before. But it was stronger now. It was the strongest I had ever heard it. In spite of myself I felt my heart leap up and begin beating hard against the smooth-worn heavy grip of my oar.

"Yes," I whispered. "Old man, I am awake."

"Of course," he said in that throaty, creaking murmur. "What wakened you?"

"Oh, old man, who knows? Hunger, perhaps. They fed us before battle. It seems a long time ago." I paused and then went on. "It is a miracle, old man, that I have developed a liking for their coarse bread and warm water. Is not that a miracle? For I was always a careful chooser of food and drink."

"No matter," he said. The eye was yet turned toward me; in the pale glimmer—it might have been moonlight, though I had never observed moonlight so clear and searching as this—the eye blazed with life. I wanted to tell him he seemed to me in that instant as young as any man I had ever known. But it was no place to bandy compliments, and I had my defenses to think of. For, I have thought since then, when men are trapped together—in war, in slavery, in darkness —each must keep his own invisible shield up at all times. When the shield drops away he is worse than naked; he is at the mercy of his emotions. And we Greeks, before the Romans, had learned to keep those emotions in harness. Before they stole our bodies and our truths, we were men. It was still possible to be a man if one kept the shield.

"No matter, Voldi," the old Bear was saying. I could scarcely hear him; yet the words seemed to burn my bones. "There is other food and drink. What has wakened you had wakened me. Now think." All was quiet again—only the rustle of the waters, the creak of the stern sweep and, somewhere above, a soldier laughing softly. No doubt he'd be congratulating himself on having come through another battle and a severe storm. My teeth ground together despite myself and I said, whispering hard, "I think, old man! Sometimes I think too much."

"No," he said strongly. "Think. Have you ever smelled air like this before? Or seen light like this before?"

Gradually then his words—they still seemed in my bones like fire—took hold. I turned my face to the sweep port; though I didn't raise myself again, yet as I examined the quality of the light falling through there, I could see that he was right. It was fluid as melted silver; yet it held something else. When I was a child I had observed light like that. It had been long ago, when I was seated with my father and mother and brothers, just beside the white wall of our home. The stars had been out, and each shape of bush and tree and path rim and leaf had been clearly outlined.

Cautiously, as one might test the edge of a cliff before crawling outward to an eagle's nest, I smelled the air. And again the feeling of wonder and strangeness filled me, for the air was different.

My nostrils contracted then. I said softly, "Old man, it is only that we are near land. Those are the land smells."

"Yes, land. And what else?"

Rage filled me. My hands tightened on my oar grip.

"What else must there be? Signs and portents, visions and wonders? Old man, old Bear," I said cruelly, for I could feel the shield slipping a little and I must hold it high. "One morning soon the overseers will come here and find you smiling at them. Or discover you trading your joyful words for a moment of happiness. Then they will kill you; one blow—as hale as you are, one blow. Then the short-sword and the fishes. It would amuse them. And I will tell you this, old one"—I was leaning forward, the oar grip pressing my chest—"they are fools, but in this they will be right. When there is no chance for truth to exist, to mention its name in faith and trust is a sin. It is a black sin."

I realized then that he was laughing and my rage could not hold back. He was laughing softly, but it was a real laugh. I said, "I speak as a Greek, not a soft-headed believer in hearth idols." I lifted my hands; the chained wrists felt my anger, blood pounding in them. "Let your words cut these, old man."

Even as I spoke, he had ceased laughing; and now, I thought, our friendship, such as it had been, would also stop. For I'd seen it happen before; for a time, two men would strike up a mumbled acquaintance here below. They would tell each other where they came from, their family name, and would confide small details of a past which was all they possessed. That was all very well, but what they did not know—could not know, as they grasped at these straws of comfort—was that regret and the pain of regret's poison began destroying them. Soon they would go mad, or at the least become implacable enemies. It was better if they had been enemies from the start, I had thought; for then they possessed shields, and these and these only could save them.

But the Bear was not offended. He was still looking as far toward me as his great head could turn.

"Yes, Voldi. By your lights you are a Greek. By mine you are a man and somewhat of a thinking man; one who deserves better of life than this. I think we are near shore. That much is true."

On the opposite tier of benches a man began howling like a dog gone mad, and those around him wakened and cursed; chains clanked, and the benches made that shifting sound that comes when many men stir in the agony of being wakened. From above there was a sharp word, and the sounds of footfalls on the short stair; peering along the aisle, suffering the fetid stench which was worst there, I could see the feet and legs of an overseer. But he came no farther, only remained crouched in the entryway, eyes shining in the light of an oil lamp.

The man who had been taken by nightmare quickly ceased his noise—it trailed off into a series of whimpers and then stopped utterly. Somebody on the first bank of rowers cursed the overseer, voice low but savage. I could hear the overseer laugh. It was a satisfied laugh. He slapped his whip at the wall of the hatchway; it made a sound like an oar breaking. Then he went up again, footfalls soft and softer.

Somehow sight of him had made solid the weight in my chest. It was not my heart, though that was beating almost richly enough to suffocate me. It was something else, part of what I have called my shield, perhaps; I do not know what it was. But it was as heavy with depth as a boulder no man could move. "There," I whispered. "So much for being near shore. Break him, Bear. Remove him, as you would cut my chains with words."

"Not words alone," said the Bear; and this time he made a forward motion with his head. I leaned close, the oar grip digging again into my chest muscles, and the old man said, "Words and very simple action. Now, Voldi, listen."

I understood as I listened that I had never truly listened before. Oh, I had thought of his words; had considered what he had told of that battle of Actium, in which Antony lost to Octavian, and in which, more vastly important to me, galley slaves had gone free. But what had an event thirty-one years past to do with the present? Yet, as he spoke now, all I had worked to put down and forget rose up again in me; I must confess it, I was no true Greek then. My veins began working with a yeast of triumph; it seemed to me, with one part of my person, that madness lay just beyond the next thought. My thoughts richened and grew like a boy's when he thinks for the first time of the world before him, with its infinite chances.

I could feel the shield slip and slip; I grunted, nodded from time to time, attempted—in a desperate clutch after the slipping shield—to throw dark reason into his shining plan. Yet I could not. And it was not all so unreasonable. There was a drunkenness in me, though I had not had a draught of unmixed wine for more than a year; there was a feeling of forward-going, as though something that shone in the light were about to release me like an arrow. When I heard this thing, I thought the old man was a kind of sorcerer; so simple was the plan, yet it needed so much to assist it.

So he talked on, while the light shone and the drum-beats sounded; craning there, I had ceased to protest even with grunting objections. Again as we sat in that clear light from the ports I thought, beneath the sense of his words, of my past life; of the way the grass had shone beneath my sandals. Of the temple where my mother had gone on the holy days to make little sacrifices for the peace and health and joy of our family; of the colonnades, some of them broken, others proud, of our ancient places of worship. The voices of the Romans at their games were like the voices of crows; but my mother's, at her worship, had been a dove's. My hands clenched over the oar grip, and the sweat that dripped from my forehead was not in the weather, for there was coolness on the water, and the still light shone.

Then at last the old man we called the Bear ceased to talk and waited. I said, "It has come to me, old man. The knowledge that I would rather die in the attempt than live as I have for a year gone on living. Breath without freedom is dead in the lungs. It stinks in the throat. Up to now"—it was hard saying, but I had to inform him; though possibly, it comes to me now, he knew—"up to now I have owned a shield." He nodded. I said, "It served as my armor against madness; it guarded me from the helpless thoughts of those who dare to hope. But——" I was breathing more slowly, and the racing tide of my blood had calmed. He nodded again. I went on, "But that itself is, I see, a sort of madness. I do not know how others in the past have felt concerning slavery. I do not see now— though in the past I thought I had seen—how any man born could be a good slave. A good slave!" I laughed —only a little. And he was laughing as well. "Well, well, then," I said. "You have my apology for being born a fool."

He said, "Wait. Wait, now. I will tell Diarno, on the bench ahead of me." And he nodded once more, slowly, as if we had all the time in the world; as if the sand in the hourglasses, the water in the water clocks, were not falling and floating. I felt the same. I felt that the same light would come in through those ports forever; that until we willed it, the dawn with its cries and alarms, its crowing of the pet fighting cocks the officers kept in cages for their amusement, would never come. So I sat back, watching my hands on my oar grip; they were lightly clenching now, and for the first time since I had come to this place— save in broken dreams—I was at peace.

And yet it was not a safe plan. No soldier alive whose existence depended on it would have thought it foolproof. We had no maps scrolled out, no definite campaign deploying this man here, that one there. We had a battered multitude upon whom we might, if the gods smiled, depend; Jason in his magic ship had safer protection! And as for our men, they were all in chains. Yet I must tell this too: the structure of the ship, its heaviness and substance around me, did not seem to be there. It was as if the known world were weightless and also as if I could, a little, see through it into something beyond. I lifted my head and mumbled what I could recall of the prayers my mother had always made to her important gods. As I did so I was astonished to see the circles of iron still clamping my wrists. They seemed to have no place there; to be figments of my thought, unimportant and not encumbering me. Ahead, the old Bear had succeeded in wakening Diarno; I could hear them in low converse. I could make out their bare outlines in that light.

The wonder of that light! Sometimes it comes back to me at untoward moments; when I am only walking down my village street, an old man now, and with my mind on something else—there it is, quick and flashing like the look you catch, slanting, in the eye of a child; but sustained and lasting long. I do not think it is a simple light to find. And yet it comes most simply and when it is not expected. It has appeared to me often and clearly since.

I sat in it then and waited; and presently, in the timeless slowness of all around me, the Bear leaned back once more and murmured. "Now." Only the word; it was enough. For I stood, crouching as high as I could in my chains, and gave a great roar fit to bring down all the Roman false gods in a black-winged fury. At the selfsame moment the Bear stood and roared at the top of his lungs; and smaller Diarno, beyond him, was upon his feet, clutching as we did at the chains, shaking them and calling.

I tell you it was a sound. All around us the half-sleeping men stirred and jangled their chains, cursed and reviled us—for such a noise brings out the most grim, whimsical side of overseers and officers and captain. Then, when I saw the overseer's lamp, this time come bobbing in haste down the stair, I stopped the noise and sat once more. He had seen me, no doubt of it; I was the last of us three to slump back in my chains. Around us all tumult ceased also, as the overseer, lamp flashing high, pounded down the aisle way. Through near-shut eyes I could see him as he raised the whip in his right hand—they are strong, these Roman half-servants, and they have their own sense of rough justice. Yet his voice seemed to me thin and unworldly.

The whip fell upon my shoulders. It fell, and fell, and fell again. Through the lashing, through his voice, angry and full of its self-importance, I watched the light which did not alter. And surely the gods are wondrous when they arrive, for I only pitied him. To be sure I pitied him even a shade more when the Bear, rising in front of me, reached and managed to drag the overseer within a tremendous grip of forearms. But that had been in the plan, to anger this overseer—in a year you know a man well, at least on the outer side, and can gauge what he will or will not do—and it was falling out as it should have. I must tell, too, that I was not surprised. This overseer was the same who, a month before, had tortured the man on the bench in front of Diarno until he drove that one to madness; there is rough justice in all of life, it seems. And fortunately the Bear had clutched him in the proper position for breaking a neck, so that there was no outcry. The lamp had been knocked down; it burned for a little and then went out with a splutter and some mild smoking. After that we worked in the shadows, while the light through the sweep ports stayed as it had before. All along the banks of crouching men it went its way, touching an eye here, a curve of knotted shoulder there. A great gentle light; remembering my mother's gods, I wished the soul of the overseer well on its journey through the dark underworld. When we were done with him in the shadows and had his short-sword, little Diarno said in the voice of an agitated reed, "Hit with the blade, strike off your chains!"

But the Bear's voice was strong and reaching as the duumvir's drums above deck. "We will not blunt the blade on our chains, Diarno." The Bear was standing as high as he could in his chains; he held the sword, it glittered in the calm light. He spoke to the banks of rowers; all were awake now, turning and watching, waiting. "I have the overseer's sword!" he called. "If we stand together—all of us pulling to the limit of our strength—we can break these benches. We outnumber overseers and soldiers. I will walk up the stairs in the lead, using the sword, so that if there is more blood-letting, mine will be the blood first spilled. And now, come!" Suddenly his voice rang and was

greater than the duumvir's drums. "Stand, pull for
life and freedom as did those slaves under the decks
at Actium!"

Of course it had been done before. Slaves in the
galleys had pulled up their benches in the past. Yet for
so long had it been a blind and empty dream to these
men that, as the Bear's words ceased ringing, there
was at first only an echoing growl and mutter among
them—but I was standing, straining on the chains;
Diarno was standing. Then I could see a scrawny-
necked, knob-shouldered wreck of a man in front of
Diarno, also standing; and the murmur was growing
to a shout, and more were upon their feet. In the
wood of the benches to which the chains were attached came a slight shudder. Now the strain on the
circles of iron around my wrists was intolerable, as
though it would cut my hands off. I knew every man
was feeling it, and there was no time for cheering or
shouting; only for the vast, concerted effort.

And then with a rending crash a bench came up,
splintering and cracking as it came; and another; and
just when I had felt that my bench was of iron rooted
to stand forever, the heavy but rotted and sea-water-
spoiled timber yielded, groaned, and my hands flew
high, the chains jangling together as the bench wood
flew to strike my back with jagged edges. I noted no
pain; only that the light was as steady, as full and
serene as it had been. I marveled a little that these
benches, built to withstand just such an insurrection,
had finally broken; yet to tell the truth, I marveled
more at the serenity of the light. For in those moments—as, all around me, more benches cracked, split,
as more men stood to their full height—I felt that any
man alive can do anything he truly wishes to do. Often
I still feel that. It is a feeling beyond jubilation. It has
to do with calm, with strength, with a silent light.

We were a strange, bedraggled army—dragging
stumps of benches from our arms, wedges of wood
that swung heavily, we stood high and free—walking
into the aisle, clambering down from the ports, leaving those accursed oars. We were a strange awkward

army, but there was strength in us as fierce as any army at Thermopylae. And as more and more of us stepped into the aisle, and as there was noise above decks—a cry, a shout, the running of feet, the signals that the officers had heard us and would meet us above the hatchway—Diarno and I took our places just behind the Bear at the head of this slow-footed, freedom-breathing army. The sword glittered in the Bear's right hand. The chains that swung from his wrist did not impede the clean strength of that hand. Chains, too, could be weapons; it came to me that all of us were well-armed. Just behind me a dark little man with one eye said, peering forward and up to the hatchway stairs, "I am not crying from fear, friend. It's not fear! But I had never thought to be standing upright again. I had never thought it!"

We were moving forward now, the Bear, then Diarno and I, then the rest at our backs. As we reached the hatchway steps, carrying our chains, the duumvir's drums sounded out above us. The tip of the sword in the Bear's right hand reached into the light pouring down those steps. It was like an answer to the drums. I knew, watching it, that soon the drums would be silenced; yet, though I had always, as I've said, hated the duumvir and the idea of the time-keeping drums most of all, yet now there was no hate in me. It was past hate. It was very quiet. It was justice and need. Watching the Bear, too, as we climbed on—there they were, ringing the hatchway, a dozen or twenty soldiers, their swords ready, their armor on, their faces set in that cascade of brilliant light—watching the Bear as I also watched these soldiers, I had the thought that he would have made a great gladiator. But then he was a farmer and not a believer in that sort of fighting. He was a man and no skilled beast. That was part of the reason why they could not stop us. They had precision and the art of arms on their side. We had nothing but ourselves and one sword and the chains and the bench ends—and our terrible need.

The first soldiers leaped; the Bear swung his sword; I was attacked from the left, and was flailing with my chains, with all my released strength. From the hatchway poured the rest of our men, streaming up and up, pouring out to cover the deck—even then, in the maelstrom of blows and blood and shouts and the swarming blindness of battle, I noted how the vast light shone. It was not a soft light. It was gentle, but very strong. It seemed to me then that it stood beyond battle, beyond the raging shadows on the deck boards, as though it contained and cupped the final truth of battle and all man's striving. We fought on.

They fought well, I suppose, those soldiers. Their captain—he was astoundingly young—was very valiant. He would gladly have died rather than bear the ignominy of enduring an escape of the galley slaves from a ship under his command. Yet they had fought one battle that day and had been in a storm afterward. I have thought much, since then; I know how they felt; I can, perhaps, sympathize. We were too many for them; at the first there was bloodshed, and some of our men went down, and some of theirs. But even then, at the first, you could tell how it would end. Yet there was a mystery past all this; I think somehow that they felt it too. I think it slowed their sword arms and gave pause to their trained rushes and bitter sallies.

Later—oh, it seemed much later, though it appeared to me that the light in the sky would stand forever, and that whatever dawn came after it would be like no other dawn yet seen—we had conquered them. We had bound them hand and foot; had laid the bodies of the dead apart for decent burial. And, though you would think the utmost vengeance would live among our men and that, even with the Bear commanding us, we would not leave a soldier or an overseer alive —this was not so. It, too, was part of the mystery. I have no easy words for it. Yet it was there, moving among us, bound into the light which seemed part of our bones and bellies. I am an old man now, yet even today I have not answered the questions that came to me then as, after the battle, after the silencing of the duumvir's drums, I walked with the Bear on deck. We stood in the stern, near that high-curved sweep of wood. Its shadow was a swan's throat on the hushed water. And again I smelled the land—it smelled of olive trees and beautiful darkness; it was not far off past this deck.

After we had rested a little and before the morning came, we would finish striking off all of our chains and would row for shore. That had been decided. But now the questions leaped on my tongue.

"You were right," I said. "I have never smelled land like this one. Where are we, then, old Bear?"

He was leaning on the bulwark, watching the light on the water. He said, "I have smelled this land before in other seasons. I could not forget it, Voldi. I came here with my father when I was very young. There" —he gestured—"is the edge of Egypt; and this, before us, is Palestine. And we are near Jaffa, off the Palestine coast." He plucked at his chin and stared into the sky. You could see where most of the light came from. It came from a single star. I remember its light. Where are there words to say it all? It was a young rose, and the fire in the blood of youth, and the new air of morning, and the end of countless years. "There was a town, Bethlehem, they called it the House of God. They waited for a sign in the sky—I remember well. The sign would tell them of the birth of a king." He stopped; then went on. "Voldi, that star is the sign; I think it hangs near the town, near that Bethlehem."

I did not answer. I could tell that he could answer no more of my questions, so I asked no more then. We only went on looking at the star. Sometimes I think I still see it—that it has never gone out.

Bounty Hunters

BY DON TROMPETER

THE DOE was a half-mile off the shore, and moving over the ice slowly, with her weakened legs spraddled to hold her balance. Now, knowing her fate, she paused in the drifts and threw her head over her shoulder to sniff of the wolves still concealed in the thick strip of pine and balsam up on the ridge.

I put the glasses on the back compartment and settled the automatic between my knees.

"They'll be out in a few seconds," I said.

Jamie gave a nod, and made a steep turn away from the floundering doe, into the frost-aureoled sun, into the citrine flashing of color over the snow and the white-capped evergreen. Wisps of cloud lay in ribbons over the chill land, and reflections of land and ice not visible from our height seemed imprinted along them.

We went back along our route and crossed the trail of the doe, and the wolf tracks, and passed over the six deer lying in the snow at the edge of the slope leading into the tamarack swamp below. Frost hung like smoke over the animals, and obscured all but the tall, spired tips of the dark tamarack. A small buck with its left antler broken off jumped to its feet and pushed down a birch with the weight and pressure of its chest, and began to nibble the frozen bark and buds.

"Make a nice film," I said.

Jamie shrugged. "Except that——" he began.

"Yeah," I said. The doe was approaching closer and closer to the waiting wolves.

The frost and sun and the bitter cold combined to set the world aflame. It was gold and saffron and pink and amber. To our left, displacing the topsy-turvy map of lake and timber we could not see, there rode the reflection of our plane, like a ghostly companion on this mission of death. I wondered idly if it cast its own shadow out somewhere beyond. The six deer were now behind us, bathed in a golden glow of sun and sparkle off the frost riming every bush and tree.

Over the lake the clouds and frost were thinning. The doe floundered a mile ahead and the seven wolves were out of the forest and trotting easily in its trail. The glitter of snow was minimized at this angle and the shadow of the plane rode far beyond the wolves, seemingly bounding across the rise of drifts brushed with the yellow of sun.

"She's stopped now," I said. "Jamie? She's just standing out there."

Jamie had eased the throttle and I knew what his inclinations were before he spoke.

"Should we jump them now?" Jamie asked. "We'll lose most of the pack, but the doe might get away. We might get one or two anyway. What do you think, Christian?"

I waited a moment on that one. I would not have to make any decision in a couple more seconds. The doe was motionless, with her head down and her legs spraddled unnaturally, very far apart, and her flag pressed against her rump. Abject, utterly defeated— and from the air-distance, looking down, she was frightfully isolated and tiny. Then I heard the cry of the wolves as they spread apart. It is a kind of quavering protest, and yet an affirmation of the need to kill and to endure, which seems to rise from a primitive and universal grief that leaves one shaken with a sense of inexpressible isolation.

A black wolf and three lighter ones that looked like big police dogs raced toward her from the right flank, while the others, closing in from the left, had already struck her at least once, and had brought her floundering onto her belly. I set the binoculars onto the storage compartment.

Jamie turned his head. "Too late now," he said.

We hooked open the window, and I pulled on my gloves, and settled my cap down over my ears.

"The eyes okay?" Jamie asked.

"They're okay," I answered.

"Fine," Jamie said. "Then, here goes nothing."

I got the roller-coaster sensation as the bottom seemed to fall out of the plane, then the lift as the plane leveled off and the air moved over the wings as it was meant to do. I crept onto my knees and forced a leg under my buttocks and pushed the shotgun barrel past Jamie's shoulder. I held my face close to Jamie's neck to avoid the slipstream biting into my eyes and blinding them with tears.

A wolf was streaking through the snow at top speed, tail straight and level with its head. It was a blur of power and speed, and the shoulder and flank muscles moved under the splendor of a shiny coat of tan and yellow hair.

"Good enough?" Jamie asked. We were a little ahead of the beast, but as we dropped it gained on us. The plane gave off that abnormal, grinding noise, which I sometimes felt, leaning out the window with the upper part of my body into the blast of wind and cold, might be coming from deep in my intestines. I forced the barrel into the slipstream, and when it swung past his wet black nose I squeezed off the trigger, and thus answered Jamie's question by the blast of the gun and the dying yelp down in the snow. Jamie leveled off just before the skis struck, and the somersaulting wolf, splaying blood into the bright prisms of frost, struck the wing-tip with its limp hind paws. Its jaws snapped shut on air, and death ended its somersault.

I pushed shells into the magazine. "Get her loaded?" Jamie asked.

"Loaded." The skis struck the snow, and we were going to taxi after this one. He was running with a hind quarter of the doe in his jaws. He was gray and tan, and heavy black fur ridged his thick back. He was undoubtedly a wolf out of the north, from up among the caribou. Snow spurted from under his tan belly and scattered over his tail and tracks. When the barrel moved beyond the meat I pulled the trigger. The meat didn't drop from his jaws, and I knew I had Judas'd him with a poor shot that struck him toward the tail.

Jamie tilted us onto the right ski, until I thought the wing would dig the wolf and the meat off the ice, and until I had the sensation that I could have snatched the meat from the wolf, had my arms been a little longer. There was no missing him this time, and the meat dropped, and the wolf ploughed a considerable furrow through the snow, pushing the meat along.

The skis struck a drift, and we were thrown into the air by the rebound and, with full power, Jamie maneuvered toward the distant shore and the four wolves heading for the rocks and timber. When he put us onto one which was churning snow on the shore, I knew the others would get away, unless we happened to run across them again when they emerged from the timber into another lake.

There were huge boulders along the shore, and thick cedar beyond, and between the boulders the drifts had piled heavily. This wolf—he was almost entirely black—floundered for an instant when the snow between two boulders gave way. He was thrown onto his back, and just as he regained his footing and started up the ridge I fired twice at his shoulders and saw him flatten.

But we had gone in a little too close. Jamie had made one of the miscalculations which no artist can afford to make, even though he might take the risk. The right ski struck high on the shore and Jamie used the rudder to try and complete a turn onto the ice. We careened off the rocks, and before the turn was completed the wing-tip struck with full force against a rotten tree and showered the area with bark and wood as the trunk snapped. The impact threw me over Jamie, and my face into the combing, before

I was thrown back. Jamie cut the power, and we scrambled out.

The leading edge of the wing was indented for about twelve inches, but there seemed to be no damage at all to the ski or bracing. Jamie ran his hand along the metal and scarred paint and shook the wing to see if it had loosened where it joined the fuselage.

"Nice tough piece of airplane," I said.

Jamie had a frown on his handsome face. "I guess it's okay," he said.

I was about to say something in regard to the smashed feeling in my skull, but then I heard the black wolf snarling up in the bank and knew I had Judas'd another beast for today, and had about had my fill of it. I got my Luger out of the back and walked under the wing, and thought I would give humor a feeble attempt. It was feeble, all right. It froze in the air and dropped underfoot. "Next time we'll cut wood with an ax," is what I said, which is rather stupid, but not skirting around anything in the way of criticism; for I understood, perhaps reluctantly, that death was a debt for living, and that sooner or later a man also Judas'd himself. What I felt angry about, I guess, was this black wolf snarling in the snow.

I climbed the bank in a whirling snowstorm, for Jamie had started the engine and was beginning to taxi out to bring in the heads of the wolves around the deer. The blown snow behind him on the lake was full of sun-gold, and the ravens were moving around the slain doe. They danced in and out of the body cavity and fought one another for scraps, and the glint of light off their wings mirrored all the way in to shore. Jamie had stopped now, a small figure at the distance, and was leaning over the wolves to do his work.

The ravens were croaking way out there, and I heard the brittle, twenty-below-zero voice of the frozen wilderness, a subdued crackling of wood splitting and ice reverberating, and snow falling off burdened boughs, and through all this I heard my heart thumping and saw my breath vaporizing, and from the hard rock cores on the slope there came those snarls of pain and hate which seemed to burn out of the billion-year-old granite on either side of them.

He was very alive, but immobilized by what appeared to be a spinal wound. He did, however, turn his sleek head toward me. Some snow had melted on his back, and his hide glistened like jet or rubbed soot. His wide-spaced eyes were of the deep yellow color of a birch leaf in fall, and as filled with light and refractions of light. His snarls coiled around those boulders like a whip around a man's soul.

His eyes did not follow my pistol, but remained on my face. I lowered the gun and stumbled around the rocks, because something forbade my finishing the kill until I had confronted him.

He gave a feeble lunge when I came toward his head. In the background were Jamie and the delicate beauty of the red and white plane, with a whirring blade and the dots of carcasses and the living specks of fighting ravens, and the sack which Jamie dragged from place to place out there.

There was something in those wide open eyes which I tried to read, without projecting, and things I tried to see in them which I could not see. If you ever sit you down in a comfortable sunny slope in the fall of the year, and gaze continuously into the branches of the forest, you will get a great many impressions of light and life and, of course, much of it too will come from the windless rustle of the leaves. But most of what you feel will come from inside your heart and soul, and so I could not claim that every man will feel the same things. But there will be certain universals, and when you have finished gazing into the sunlight on those leaves and watching and listening and feeling, you will rise a little stiffly, and there will be a universal sadness and melancholy in your heart, seeing this captured fire and inevitable ending of the leaves falling and becoming clay and dust. But some of the fiber of sun and sky and cloud and light that disappears with the death of those leaves will also be in you, and you will wait until the next autumn season, and, when the leaves turn, the ache to see and feel once again will move in your soul. You will not feel complete enough to endure another winter until you have once more looked upon this eternal light and fire and death.

So I stared at the wounded wolf, knowing that there was no force on earth which could prevent my destroying the lights in the eyes from which no hate gleamed, the brain which signaled no fear, no passions of any kind directed at me. A corner of my mind recalled a Balzac story about the Legionnaire who betrayed his strange companion in the green beauty of an oasis out on the fire of the Sahara. It was not bounty money which had brought either of us to this moment of dying. Out there on the Sahara the Legionnaire had witnessed the splendor of sunsets and storms and clear night skies, and he related he had understood God.

The wolf pulled his throat out of the snow. When his lips drew back over his fangs, I saw that they were worn to the gums along the incisors, and that his seasons had taught him all there is to know about life, and that it is sacrifice.

His eyes appeared sleepy now, and not at all fiery, or furious at the leveling of the short barrel inches from his brain. I did not hear the report, or feel the slap of the butt against my palm, for his eyes closed as in sleep, and his head slumped into the snow between his paws, and I muttered, feeling the futility of my words: "Brother? I am sorry."

I brought my black wolf down from the snow and dragged its inert form over by the rotten pine, which lay broken on the rocks and ice. I pulled out buried driftwood and built a fire of dry birch and poplar, which had been cut and barked by beaver. I sat down on a length of broken pine, with my back against a boulder. Jamie was tying the gunny sack to the right strut, and the ravens, cawing mightily, heaved up and down over the doe's body.

My wolf was hardly any longer a symbol of anything. His bloody tongue hung over his yellowed canines, and a swatch of blood, already sinking into the frost from the bank downward, destroyed any suggestion of immortality. Last night my wife Meda had taken hold of my fingers, kissed them, pronounced them gentle, and had placed them along her abdomen to feel of the life stirring in our first child. Now, feeling the beat of the flames upon my face, especially the scalding feeling where I had smashed the flesh against the combing of the plane, I gathered up a fistful of melting snow by the fire and tried to cleanse my hands of blood where no blood was visible, and cursed the paradoxes of life.

Jamie taxied back at full speed, and the snow broke over the skis and fell away like waves split by the prow of a boat. The ravens fluttered in the whirl of snow behind the plane and then settled again. I threw more wood on the fire, removed my boots and watched the steam rise off my damp socks, and, when Jamie climbed out, told him to bring our lunch.

Jamie had no conflicts over the black wolf. He had not looked into its eyes. He set his mittens on the log and took his knife from its sheath and began to skin it out. And I don't suppose it makes any difference how much a piece of dead meat is violated. He severed the hide above the paws and cut along the inside of the hindquarters to the anus, did likewise with the front, and then slit along the lean belly to the tip of the black nose. In less time than it took me to pour coffee into plastic cups and impale two frozen cheese and bologna sandwiches on sticks and set them near enough to the flames so that they'd burn on the outside without ever thawing much of the cheese or meat—as campfire sandwiches always do —Jamie had peeled the glossy hide off the dark meaty form and was separating it from the hide, cutting under the ears and around the eyes, just as one skins out a beaver. He wiped his blade in the snow, rolled up the hide, and washed his hands with a view for sanitation. The nose of the wolf leaked blood into the snow, and there were a couple of purplish wounds back of the front shoulders where two of twenty-eight buckshot had injured the spine.

The heat had drawn billions of black snow fleas, no larger than grains of pepper, around the area, and they covered the sides and edges of our steaming cups. You can't do much about them, so we drank our coffee and swallowed the crusty sandwiches, and the fleas, and whatever ash had fallen onto cup or sandwich.

Several hundred ravens were gathered out on the ice, and there were thirty or forty over each carcass and as many more soaring from one spot to another. The sun was over the distant tamarack swamp, where the pack had first started the doe out of the herd on the slope, and the lake had taken on a pink and gray tone, and the tops of the distant pine flamed as if fired beyond the frost.

Jamie held another sandwich over the flames and the frost began to steam out of it, and the white bread turned black. I poured more coffee, and the snow fleas hopped around inside the rims, and a few thousand of them settled on my hands and around the melting snow where the cup made a depression. I lighted a cigarette and leaned back, and could easily have fallen asleep.

"How's the head?" Jamie asked. "You gave it a good crack."

"Fine," I answered. Jamie looked across the ice, studying something out there.

"That was pretty good shooting."

"The flying was fine, too," I said.

Jamie flushed. "We ought to run onto another wolf or two before going back."

"Maybe," I said.

"I don't think hitting the tree damaged the wing very much," Jamie said. "It will fly, okay."

"Yes," I said.

"Maybe I shouldn't have gone after this last one . . ."

"You made it," I said. "How do you like the sandwiches?"

"Fine."

The fire had eaten a depression in the ice. Embers fell into the puddle, hissed, steamed, and went out. Feeble yellow flames went out, one by one, and cold closed in around us. The wolf carcass, lacerated in a thousand places where Jamie's blade had sliced, had frozen and become frosted. Out there, the ravens, unsettled by their bounty, fluttered from one carcass to another. I tugged on my boots, dumped the coffee dregs and dead and drowned fleas out of the cups, and packed the thermos and remaining sandwiches into the plastic case.

"Ready?" Jamie asked. His eyes were reddened from sun and glare and general weariness. His dark face was lined around the eyes and at the corners of his sensitive mouth. He carried the hide under his arm like an athlete holding a football.

"I reckon I am," I said, and took up my Luger and the thermos case and went along. The fire was dead, and ice was already forming over the sunken ash and blackened embers. Jamie hesitated at the plane. I believe he had been hurt by my remark about using an ax to cut trees.

"Maybe you'd like to fly for awhile?"

I was settled in the back, with the shotgun between my knees. I pointed at the front seat. "That's your specialty," I said. "This one is mine."

Jamie fastened his safety belt. I had got out of the habit of using mine. I only had to loosen it whenever I maneuvered myself into firing position.

Jamie tugged at the starter and the beautiful little plane trembled with life from nose to wing-tip. We threw our weight around to loosen the skis and started over the snow.

I hollered into his ear above the thunder: "What would you do if there was no bounty on wolves, Jamie?"

He shrugged his wide shoulders, but he didn't speak until we were air-borne above the fighting ravens and the bloody carcasses. "I'd keep on hunting them."

"Check," I said, and settled back, and patted the automatic, and wished we would either come upon

something fairly soon, or that I could lean back into
something a little warmer than this plane, with a
double-strength hot toddy in one hand and a cigarette
in the other, by a fire, in a warm room, with a comfortable robe and slippers, and no thoughts, no cold,
no blood, not for awhile.

"How would you like a drink of brandy, Jamie?"

"Not so good."

"How about a Tom and Jerry?"

"Fine," Jamie said.

"Or a hot rum and brandy?"

"Fine," Jamie said.

The kills and the ravens were remote specks rising
out of the frost and snow a mile behind us, and ahead
and on either side a crisscross of wolf, fox, moose,
deer, and rabbit tracks led in all directions. Earlier in
the morning, we'd been in an area to the east where
there had been no tracks at all. There always are a
lot of tracks, where there are any at all, but it is sheer
luck to come upon a wolf pack, even though you
may find a dozen deer kills within a few square miles.
In February, the bachelor packs would be moving in
search of females from family packs, and some of
them would mate with them, and the males from the
family packs would join the remaining bachelors, and
there would be a good deal of activity this month,
their mating season. Then, in March, the rabbits and
hares mated, and the bucks chased the does onto the
ice, and the wolves and foxes understood this and,
since the deer are fewer by then or moving toward
the north shores of islands and lakes, where the spring
sun thaws the vegetation, the foxes and wolves wait
upon the rabbits courting on the ice. You come upon
many places in the snow where one wolf has chased
after the love-blind buck, while another has run
parallel and waited in the snow, until the doe made
her abrupt leap to one side of her pursuer—only to
find the jaws waiting for her there, while the buck,
twisting in mid-air to get back on the doe, squealed
its sacrifice at almost the same instant. You fly over
spots like that, two bloody specks in the snow, a bit of

white fluff blowing around, two sets of wolf tracks leading off.

Jamie began a circle, and I looked down and watched two otter moving across the lake in the deep snow. They left a trail more like a furrow than anything else. I was surprised to see otter out on the lake, for they generally kept to the shoreline, and preferred moving under the ice where the water level had dropped and they could travel unobserved and search for crayfish or minnows.

We went down, and I took film of them as we taxied alongside. The snow was above their depth, but they undulated through it, beautifully sinuous, and not at all afraid of us or the plane. Every now and then one or both of them stood on hind legs, back curved, and barked at us, somewhat in the manner of young seals. Their canine teeth were long and sharp. I got out and threw bits of a sandwich to them. After sniffing of the first morsel they caught all the others in the air, tossed them slightly, swallowed them, and sat back on their powerful tails to beg for more with light coughing sounds. I have never heard of another animal killing an otter, and I doubt if they have many natural enemies, beyond the greatest predator of all. Since fur prices were down, they were increasing in number, and it was common to see them around the open creeks and streams along the beaver flowages. They stood on their paws as we took off, and long afterward their furrowed trail ran back into the red and yellow glare across the lake.

I was beginning to grow weary and my eyes were aching with tension and fatigue when Jamie went into a sharp bank and began to fumble with the window. I got into position and saw a fox racing along an ice hummock toward a treeless, wind-swept reef. Its brush was out straight, and it was not wasting any time in attempting to reach the reef and whatever cover it offered.

I am not much of a shot when it comes to hitting a running fox. Much of the literature written about them is sympathetic, but though they have been immortalized for having outwitted hounds, and men on horseback, as far as I know nobody has poetized their futile efforts against men in aircraft. A fox will run a zig-zag course, and he will dart hither and yon. He presents a much smaller target than even a brush wolf. And I have a fondness for them, which possibly derives from childhood tales about wily Reynard, and the fact that they eat berries and fruit and mice, and have a beautiful brush to wrap cunningly around their delicate paws and nose in freezing weather.

Jamie banked and turned and slipped down, and maneuvered much more brilliantly than I shot. As a matter of fact, the laurels of artistry must be shared between Jamie and this little red creature racing along every protective crust of ice, every stone and boulder, every drift. My eyes blinded with tears and my face went numb. I emptied the magazine, filled it, emptied it once more, and while Jamie cursed in his mild fashion, either at my shooting or the fox's cleverness, I loaded up the third time.

I have an idea that Jamie did the correct thing in leveling off above the fox, circling it once, and failing to slip down onto the reef. For now that fox was exhausted, and it lay panting on the ice, a rusty blur in the snow and ice-shining rocks, waiting for us to come down and Judas it. I felt some of the struggle in Jamie, in the way he lost power, and then leveled off again, giving the engine all the power he had. I most certainly would have nailed the fox on this try. But Jamie flew on beyond, into the west-northwest; and, after all, perhaps some poet could eulogize this encounter between a bush-pilot and a northern fox.

Jamie turned toward some wolf tracks cutting across the lake ahead of the fox and the otter, which appeared to lead over a ridge, through sparse timber, and down onto a large lake perhaps two miles wide and thirty miles long. On every side were more ponds, lakes, creeks and beaver flowages, interlaced with trails of moose, deer, wolves, and fox. Jamie turned his dark head, and muttered, neither angry nor pleased.

"Nice shooting."

"Thanks," I said. "Nice flying."

"Are your eyes hurting?" Jamie said.

"My conscience . . ."

"Why didn't you say you didn't want to kill him? Why waste shells?" Jamie frowned.

"Why didn't you?" I asked.

Jamie laughed. He has a splendid laugh, deep, long, and without the hidden hostility concealed behind so much mirth.

We went on over the long narrow lake, and there were wolf tracks down the center, and on either side, and deer had crossed at various times since the previous day, and there was so little remaining of the carcasses of two of them that not even a raven fluttered over the red stains below.

Now the sun was becoming obscured, and clouds were gathering in the west and south, and the temperature was rising along toward zero. Once in awhile a gust of wind tossed us about, and you could see the mark of it passing along the ice, blowing a scurf of snow before it, like the foaming of a wave. It became more difficult to see the tracks and trails, without the shadow of sunlight in them, and sometimes we lost one, only to find we were following above others, perhaps days old.

We began to fly more toward the west and south, toward home, and I began to dwell more heavily on the pleasures of a warm fire and a hot toddy and a bath, and I figured it would be a pleasant evening at home, with Meda, and a fire in the fireplace she and I had built, and with Jamie, and the rooms darkened, except for the lights we would put on the little spruce I had brought home for Christmas, and I would watch Meda place the decorations on the tree, in the beautifully careful way she has of doing things, and drink my drinks, and Jamie would watch her, also, having his drinks and his thoughts, in his quiet manner. And the baby in Meda's womb, almost full term, having its peculiar kind of warm and peaceful evening.

My eyes were beginning to feel relieved from the lack of glare when Jamie turned toward a small lake to the south and pointed his forefinger at a single wolf which I had already noticed. It had begun to snow, though not yet heavily; a few miles south the thicker stuff was obscuring hills and timber.

We went down after the single. He seemed frantic with fear, a small wolf, standing on his hind legs and pawing at the propeller, then dropping down to dart away from us, his sharp yelps somehow smothered by the dusk and snowfall. He was such easy meat that I did not feel like killing him, but I did my duty, and he fell backward.

We stood by him until he ceased quivering. He was this year's whelp, a male. The snow was driving fast and thick now, and you could not clearly define the shoreline, less than a quarter-mile away. We threw him in the back, under my feet, and I rode with my knees jammed into my chin, smoking cigarettes in preference to inhaling the powerful rank odor of the animal.

There was nothing now to watch, for air and land seemed one, with no depth, no distance, no visibility at all. I finished the cold coffee in the thermos, unloaded the gun, and in my mind went home to Meda and the fire and the comfort of a hot bath and a few rum and brandies. Somehow, a man seems to live only long enough to fulfill his own unique and trivial destiny.